MW00584034

THE MILK FARM

THE MILK FARM
AN EROTIC NOVEL

Luc Milne

Leyland Publications
San Francisco

Author's Note: **The Milk Farm** *is a fantasy. Neither the Pleasure Corporation nor The Milk Farm exist in real life, so far as I know. Many of the sexual practices described in the text, especially unprotected anal intercourse and the ingestion of semen, are not possible in the current health crisis and may, in fact, be dangerous for years to come. The depiction and characterization of police officers in no way reflects the actual organization or practices of real-life law enforcement agencies. I have taken pains to indicate that participation in Milk Farm activities is undertaken voluntarily by adult gay men. The sometimes coercive atmosphere of The Milk Farm arises out of these voluntary commitments. Similarly, the uses of terms such as "boy" or "kid" do not indicate underage persons but are part of current gay vocabulary indicating common psychological role-playing in relationships and sexual games among male homosexuals. I think that in a different world The Milk Farm might be plausible, but at present the book should be treated by its readers as an elaborate fiction—a slightly obsessive sexual daydream—and read for pleasure and for imaginative sexual stimulation.*

Luc Milne

THE MILK FARM is copyright © 1997 by Luc Milne.
All rights reserved. Except for brief passages quoted in a newspaper, magazine, radio, or television review, no part of this book may be reproduced in any form or by any means, electronic or mechanical, including photocopying and recording, or by any information storage, computer or retrieval system, without permission in writing from the publisher.

First edition 1997
Front cover photo copyright © 1997 by Terry Studio
Cover design by Rupert Kinnard

ISBN 0-943595-61-4
Library of Congress Catalogue Card #96-78065

Leyland Publications
P.O. Box 410690
San Francisco, CA 94141
Complete illustrated catalogue available for $1 ppd.

excerpt from
THE MILK FARM
MEMBERS' HANDBOOK

Congratulations on your acceptance into the ranks of The Milk Farm client-members. This Handbook will give you an overview of The Farm's services and activities, as well as providing a guide to Milk Farm policies.

On your introductory visit to The Farm you probably saw only a small portion of the pleasures that we offer. On every visit you make we hope you will encounter new and exciting experiences.

Please remember that you are allowed to bring one guest to The Farm for a maximum three-night visit each quarter, but that the guest must be "vetted" first by our Security Division. The only exception to this rule is that you may bring guests between the ages of eighteen and twenty-one years as often as you want, as we like to see young men mingling with the client-members.

You may also propose names for membership, but the Management asks that you be discreet and careful in discussing The Farm with men whom you do not know well. The presence of any member of the media for any purpose other than private pleasure could have very unfortunate results.

CHAPTER ONE

The Milk Farm E-Mail File

OUTGOING E-MAIL FILE
 Manager, The Milk Farm
 TO:CEO.PleasureCorp@Head.private.
 FROM:MGRJack@MFarm.private.
 [Encrypted message]
 Dear Sir:
 As Chief Executive Officer of the Pleasure Corporation, you
have indicated that you wish to be notified immediately of poten-
tially serious problems in any of the Corporation's branches. I
show below some excerpts from an audio tape confiscated from
a supposed candidate for membership during his introductory tour
of The Milk Farm.

*   *   *

[Edited transcript]
Voice of Milk Farm Manager:
 "Grab his arms! Get the 'cuffs on him. . . . Now, now, don't
get excited, Mr. Brock. We just want to see what you've got in this
pocket. Well, well, what do you know? A little tape recorder
. . . and it's running too. Why don't we just set it down here on
my desk and let it run during our talk. Give me his billfold, Max,
and strip him down. . . . Quit your squawking or I'll gag you,
understand?
 "Well, your name really is Clay Brock, but what's this press card
here? You wouldn't be a member of the media, would you, Mr.
Brock? I thought you told us you were a stock broker. Why would
a reporter want a membership tour of The Milk Farm, unless he
was planning to write an unauthorized story about us?
 "Don't bother to uncuff him to get the shirt off. Just let it hang
from his wrists. Pull down those Calvin Kleins and let's see what
he's got. . . . Ah, very nice. Big plump milkballs and a good-
looking teat. Jack him up, Max, and give those nuts a little
squeeze. . . . Shut your hole, fuckface, or we'll shut it for you.

"I'll have to check him out further on the database. Meanwhile I think we'll give him a little taste of what it's like to be mancow here at The Farm. And, listen, Mr. B., we'll be taking lots of pictures and lots of video—a complete record of your first visit to us. Later, if you check out, and do become a legitimate client, we'll keep them for insurance. We don't mind having a member of the press as a customer, but we don't want him writing juicy stories about what goes on here, especially when he comes in under false pretenses and makes me waste my time giving him a tour of the place so he can get it down on a fucking tape recorder.

"I think we'll put the vacu-pump on just the head of his meat for a couple of hours—get it all pink and puffy. Then take him around the bar during the cocktail hour and let the members suck him a little. But don't let him cum. That's my personal treat tonight when I interrogate him. And gag him. I'm tired of hearing him bleat.

"Don't pump his balls. Just put a two-inch stretcher on 'em and tell the guys in the bar to jerk 'em good while they taste his milk-teat. And keep his legs spread. . . . *Spread 'em, Nutbitch! Let me see those milkbags swing!* Give him a whack across the butt. Make him keep his crotch thrust forward. He's got to learn to stay wide and open.

"After I've questioned him tonight, and taken his first load, I'll decide what to do with him tomorrow. We might have a breakfast auction and offer him as raw meat to the highest bidder. I think that guy from Texas said he likes to milk a "wild cow" once in a while. Then on Sunday we'll think up some other surprises for him. I have a notion he could be hooked up to the mechanical milker and completely drained. Then we'll send him into the dining room that night to do crotch service at the big table. If he's ever going to become a regular member, we might as well see what kind of a mouth he's got.

"See, I knew this stud had potential. His sexteat just gets bigger and bigger, the more I talk. Take him away. . . . Oh, and shave him. I intend to get my lips right down to the base of that pole and I don't want any pubic hair in my teeth. And be sure to buttplug him. Use a number four, and clean him out first. Get one of those plugs we can insert a vibrator into: I may want to play around with him, while I pull him tonight.

"And listen, guys, if this cow has squirted one drop of milk before I get him back, I'll beat your nuts black and blue."

[End of edited transcript]

*   *   *

I hope you'll excuse the rough language, Sir, but I was pretty angry, and you can see that we could have a potential problem if this Brock turns out to be a gay, but pretty straight-arrow investigative reporter. I'm checking all available sources for information about him now, and I am notifying the Chief because I want to be sure the Police are ready to move in if we need any special help with him. I think the best thing would be to "turn" him by offering him a reduced-price membership. Or maybe I'll be able to dig up some details of his personal life that we can use to convince him to keep quiet about what he's seen here at The Farm.

I suppose, now that our operation is getting so successful and we have such a broad membership base, that we can expect more problems of this sort. We'll probably have to tighten up our screening process to improve the vetting of applicants before we even bring them for a visit. "Personal assurances" from current members, and "word-of-mouth" references are just not going to be enough.

I will keep you informed about this matter. I understand you will be spending the next month at The Last Resort. I hope you have a stimulating time. My one visit there was the high point of my life, so far,

Best Wishes,
Jack Devlin, Manager

*   *   *

OUTGOING E-MAIL FILE
  Manager, The Milk Farm
TO:CHIEF@PoliceHeadquarter.private.
FROM:MGRJack@MFarm.private.
[Encrypted message]
Chief:
I have sent by messenger a copy of the tape we took off the spy I told you about on the phone yesterday. (The messenger is a member of our staff and has a good throat, if you've got time to plug it when he makes the delivery.) We suspected Brock was a reporter when the security scan at the gate indicated he might have some

sort of recording device on him; a surveillance camera confirmed that later. I went ahead with the tour anyway, as if he were really a prospective member of The Milk Farm, and I think you may enjoy the tape: I remember very well what a kick you got out of the tour when you were first introduced to us.

We've still got the reporter in "custody." He's got a nice piece of milkmeat and he could become a valuable asset as stock if we decide to keep him. On the other hand he's thirty-seven years old, and we try not to recruit establishment types, since there's too much hassle with family and business associates pursuing their disappearance from the normal work scene too stubbornly. Fortunately this guy, Clay Brock, is separated from his wife and has no immediate family except for a stepson (the wife's kid from her first marriage, who stayed with him when she split) so there wouldn't be too much interest in his disappearance from the outside world. It turns out that the chairman of the company that owns the magazine he writes for is one of our best clients, so there is some possibility we can work through him to put pressure on the guy to keep his mouth shut about what goes on here.

Of course we could always recruit the man's stepson and condition him for service in the stalls. He's eighteen, but we'd have to wait until June because he's just finishing school. We could threaten the reporter with the photos and tapes we've taken of him engaged in some very interesting activities these last few days until he brings the stepson to us for possible recruitment. Once we have the boy, whose name is Teddy, we can hold him as a "hostage" for Brock's silence. I doubt if Brock would want it known that he'd made it possible for his stepson to enter the sex industry! Please give me your professional "police" advice about our best course of action.

That brings me to your own "runaway" nephew who you recruited for us. He's coming along very well.

According to your instructions we have vacu-pumped his milkteat for long periods, sometimes three or four hours at a time if he can take it. His penis now hangs ten inches, soft, and has a good eight-and-one-half inch circumference just below the head. To get him hard we have to use the electrical prostate prod. Hard, he stretches out to about thirteen inches. The dickhead is exceptionally big and plump. Of course, when you brought him to us, his

natural milkhead was almost six inches around, if you remember. He had exceptional natural development for an eighteen-year-old.

We've pumped his milkballs in the same way and they are always pulled down into a six-inch stretcher at night. I know you want his balls to hang lower than his dick, but I'm not sure we're going to be able to manage that.

You will recall I warned you this kind of long-term pumping tends to produce a "leaker," and that's certainly the case with Tim (in fact his Farm nickname is "Honeyboy"). He dribbles a heady syrup of spicy precum almost constantly. When he's not being milked by a client, we collect this nectar in a cum suction-cup and it is considered a great delicacy at The Cock and Ball Restaurant in town. (We have credited your account with a portion of the profits from the sale of this juice.)

Given the increasingly unmanageable size of his milk equipment, and the electrical stimulation that has to be given to get him hard and to make him shoot, he's become something of a specialty item at The Farm. Precum addicts pay a premium to suck him on a continuous hourly basis, without actual milk production.

In that regard I have a suggestion to make: if you would allow us to enlarge his cocklips as well, I think his earning potential would be greatly enhanced. He had very well-defined lips on his cumhole when you convinced him to join the organization, and of course the general vacu-pumping on the whole teat has enlarged them somewhat. But if we could attach the smallest of the suction cylinders to those curves of flesh right at the cumslit, we could bring them up so that their permanent swelling would block off the constant precum leakage. This would cause the honey to back up in the milktube and would please the precum connoisseurs who would love to force their tongues right up into those swollen lips and tease the stuff out. I have several members who would pay double milking fees for the opportunity to suck on a hose like that for a couple of hours at a time, or until their own mouths get so tired they have to stop!

And frankly I think the vacu-pumped cocklips would look very handsome on Tim's meat in its present plump state. I've noticed that whenever you are finished with him, they're always very red and bloated anyway. But maybe you prefer to continue the "enlargement" on your own! I can certainly understand that, since

nothing gives me greater pleasure than to nip and grind at a pretty pair of boy cocklips myself.

Speaking of lips, that reminds me that the last time you were here you asked whether it would be possible to pump up his tongue and his mouth lips. If you still have that in mind, it would probably be a good idea to put him through a six-week course at The Cocksuck Academy over at the SbarM Ranch first. There's no point in creating luxury sucking equipment on a kid who's only got amateur technique. We've never really tested Tim to see if he's a natural sucker. Perhaps the next time you're here we should put him through the paces. We can usually tell after a few hours of force-feeding with a variety of tools whether a guy's a born cocksucker or not. If he's not a "natural," then I think it would be a waste to pump up his lips and tongue.

It would be better to give him The Cocksuck Academy's "Throat Conditioning" treatments which deaden the gag-reflex, tone up the throat muscles, and generally ream out the gullet. That would make him a "fuckthroat" and for that you don't want a thick tongue and fat lips to get in the way. He's still a good looking lad and I'd hate to see his mouth spoiled with too much pumping. I've seen your own enormous equipment, and I think I can promise you that the vision of his cute face impaled to the root of your cock, while his conditioned throat works up and down the length of it, will make the extra cost of the cocksuck lessons and the throat-reaming worth it to you.

Psychologically he's adapting very well to Milk Farm life. His stint strung up on the wall of the toilet in the bar at the Hotel, where his meat and balls were used as face- and hand-towels by the customers, went a long way to break him of some of his surliness. He seems to accept that he's now a pleasure cow and that he's still got a long way to go before he's a "finished" product.

This brings up the question of how much larger you want us to pump him. He was about seven inches when we got him. We find that any seven-inch creamteat pumped to more than twelve or thirteen inches on a permanent basis will generally lose its ability to get hard, even with extreme electrical stimulation of the prostate. After that, a mancow has to be taught to cum "soft" if he is still to be used for milking in the stalls. Conditioning a stud to achieve a "soft-shoot" is a long process and may involve some surgical im-

plants in the milkbags. I don't know what longterm plans you have in mind for your nephew. You certainly seem to get a lot of pleasure out of using him whenever you come to visit us, although last time it took several days for the teeth marks on his shaft to disappear, which resulted in a loss of revenue to The Farm.

I should mention that one of our Swiss members with a passion for giant male-udders has offered to buy Tim for a sum which would bring us a good profit and provide you with credit here at The Farm, or at any of the other Pleasure Corporation branches for a couple of years of unlimited entertainment.

Finally, I want to thank you for your last shipment of gay meat from the prison farm. One of the guys you took out of the penal "loop" by offering him "community service" here at The Farm is a treasure. He's the blonde punk with the big, loose meat that gets beet-red when it's sucked. We expect to get him into the Milking Barn the minute his conditioning is finished. At present the Lab is trying to improve the taste of his milk. It has a "wild game" kind of flavor that is not to everyone's liking. The two others proved willing but unusable here at The Farm. One just couldn't hold his milk: he squirted almost the minute a mouth touched him, and no amount of punishment could keep him from it. But since his product is like a rich custard and since he can blast it out several times a day, we've offered him a position in The Cock and Ball kitchen where they can use him for utility cum. It's handy for them to have a quick shooter whenever Chef Louis needs some juice for his cum-sauces and prick-glazes. The other one you offered our "alternative punishment regime" to, the Latino with the small sausage and the tight little balls, just couldn't get hard no matter what we did to him. He agreed to go to The Fuck Corral at the SbarM where he's being used as a training butt. Once his hole's too sloppy for good fucking, he'll also be offered a job at the Restaurant where they'll spread him out on the bar and let the customers munch those peanuts with their cocktails before dinner. So you see we're very efficient here. All the meat is put to good use, and we're grateful for anything you can supply.

At the moment we are in need of some small-to-average size milkmeat. We're overstocked on studs with monster teats just now, and the members complain that it's too much work to get a decent mouthful of cream from some of those giants. Could you

watch the surveillance tapes from the jail showers and the prison medical inspections for some gay guys with prime four or five inch teats that we can process, by light pumping, into normal mouth-sizes?

The Lab is looking for a couple of special items. They need a big prick with long foreskin—long enough and loose enough to stretch over a sphere the size of a squash ball (don't ask why!), and they are also looking for a short, but very fat "beercan" cock. They want to experiment with "circumference pumping." That's blocking off the vacuum tube just at the cockhead so that all the swelling goes into the circumference of the dick, creating meat which is wider than it is long. Apparently they think this will have the effect of making the milk bubble up out of the cumtube, rather than shooting out, so that the whole thing can be licked and nuzzled like a big, messy, warm ice cream cone. It sounds crazy to me, but if we don't keep the Lab boys happy with their pet projects, they don't keep us happy with the "boring" work, like developing the hormone treatments for better milk production from our milking stock.

Naturally we'll continue to give you the "virgin" pull on any of the teats you send us.

Before I close I want to report that the three young gay officers you recommended as possible members have all been brought into the "club." We invited them out for an overnight visit, gave them the tour, and introduced them to some of the other members. We didn't let them do any milking in the Barn. We just let them watch, up-close, in the stalls. Their eyes just about popped out of their heads, and their dicks *did* pop out of their pants! One of them, Jesse, is a very hot number. After his tour, he went straight back to his room and called the front desk for a Room Boy. He jumped the kid the minute he stepped into the room, pushed him down on the bed, straddled his chest, and shot about a quart of cop-cream over the kid's face. We got it all on the surveillance video-tape, which I'm sending along with the audio tape from the spy reporter. You'll note that the new close-up feature works great: you feel like you've got your face right down there at action-level.

After he creamed the boy, Jesse felt so guilty he helped the kid up and took him into the bathroom where he started to wipe the jizz off his face with a washcloth. But while he was doing that, he

got so hot again that he pushed the boy down to his knees and shot another hot wad down his throat. After that he seemed to go a little batty. He dragged the lad back to the bed and sat on his face for almost an hour, trying to stuff both his dick and his balls into the boy's mouth at the same time, and rubbing his asshole all over the little guy's mug. (See the last part of the tape.)

We're beginning to think that Jesse might make a better *cow* than a *client*! What about assigning him for some "special duty" one weekend a month here at The Farm?

Of course, all three of the guys said they couldn't afford the high fees on a cop's salary, but we made it clear that it is very important to us to have friends in the Police—so important that we offer them memberships and services at an 80 to 90 percent discount. (I didn't tell them that we'd actually have taken them for free!) Now that the land The Farm is on has been annexed by the city, our ties to you and to the police force are even more crucial. We're still keeping up our liaison with the county Sheriff's Office, though, because, as you know, the SbarM Ranch and The Cocksuck Academy are still outside the city limits. Our infiltration into the Sheriff's Patrol is very good. About 30% of the current officers and staff have used one or more of our facilities, mostly on a guest basis. The Sheriff himself has a "Wildgame Night" scheduled for five of his buddies at The Cock and Ball Restaurant next week.

Why don't you come out this weekend? We could play "Interrogation" with our reporter friend and have some fun with your nephew. He whimpers a little whenever we tell him you're due for a visit!

See you soon,
Jack

*   *   *

INCOMING E-MAIL FILE
　Manager, The Milk Farm
TO:MGRJack@MFarm.priv.
FROM:CHIEF@PolHead.priv.
[Encrypted message]
Dear Jack,
I'm on my way to meeting with the pussy faces on the Police Commission in a little while, but I want to take a few minutes to reply to your last message.

This is my advice about the reporter. Make fucking sure his stepson is of legal age and when he graduates in June give him a weekend at The Farm and bring him into stock. I agree that should guarantee the bastard's silence. I'll see to it that my people here give the kid's disappearance the regular bullshit treatment if anyone should report him "missing." But I think you'd better get a little extra insurance as well. On that first weekend visit, why not get some good video of him eating his own kid's meat. I have a feeling from listening to the tape of his visit, especially the part at the end when you stripped him and played a little rough with him, that he won't need a lot of encouragement to drink a load of teenmilk. If the kid is uncut, I'll milk him myself when he's ready. You know how I like a really young uncut teat full of virgin boygush. *But remember what I told you about bringing underage kids into stock.* Not even my office can protect you from prosecution if you do that.

Now, about my "runaway" nephew Tim. I have several instructions. I'm sorry that I haven't made myself clear before now.

1. I don't care if he loses his hard-on permanently once he's pumped to twelve inches or more. In fact, I want him pumped just as far and as fat as he'll go. Nothing's too big, for my purposes. If you could get him up to a steady fifteen inches of spongy milkteat, that would be great.

2. BUT I do want him to continue to give milk, and lots of it. *Do whatever you have to do to ensure that he continues to produce a high-grade cream.* It doesn't have to squirt out: a nice steady ooze will do just fine. If you have to insert small electrical buzzers at the base of his cumtube to make this happen, then just do it!

3. DON'T sell his extra precum honey to The Cock and Ball. I want it. Collect it and give it to the Lab. Ask them to make it up into gel capsules that I can pop onto my tongue during the day. As they dissolve, those little bursts of cumflavor will help to keep the memory of my sweet Honeyboy (great name!) fresh.

4. *Don't tell me you can't get his balls to hang down below the head of his meat!* At the least I want them *even* with the head. Use eight-inch stretchers if you have to. And I want his milkeggs pumped individually so they swell to maximum size, but no saline injection. I want the kid's teat and bags so big he'll have to wear a body harness just to hold them up. He's never going out

in public again anyway, so it doesn't matter if there's no designer underwear big enough to contain his equipment.

5. About his cocklips, I know what you mean. They would look very tasty vacu-pumped up a quarter-inch or so, but, as you say, I'd rather take care of that little bit of "remodelling" with my own teeth and lips and in my own good time. I like to listen to his moans when I nibble at those puffy morsels. Find a small dick-plug, if you're worried about the leakage. I wouldn't mind if his cumhole was reamed out a little bit anyway. I like to fuck down into it with the hard tip of my tongue when I milk him.

6. You're probably right about not pumping his face lips and his tongue. When I face fuck him, I usually straddle his head in a 69 position and drive down into his throat, with my balls draped over his eyes, so I can't really see much of that cute little jizzface anyway. The Throat Conditioning sounds like a very good idea. But don't hold back. I don't want his gag-reflex just *suppressed*, I want it *gone*! Give his throat muscles some extra calisthenics if you can, so they will squeeze me good. When I take him back from you, I plan to spend a lot of time with my hammer all the way down his throat, while I go to town on his teat and his bags. I've already found that if I manhandle his meat good, he instinctively opens up his gullet and lunges his lips up against the base of my prick. He may not be a "natural" cocksucker, but he sure knows how to eat you when his nuts are in a vise!

7. I've been thinking that we'd better start working on his tits. I want his nipples to stand up like juicy strawberries, about an inch high and about four inches circumference around the base of the cone. And I want them a permanent rosy color. What do you recommend? Vacu-pumping or silicone injections—or both? I like those little emery boards you use on the Room Boys' nipples to keep them tender. Make sure Tim's nips get some light "sanding" on a daily basis.

8. Tell the Swiss billionaire sucker who wants to buy Tim that I might consider a lease deal for two months out of every year if we can agree to terms. And after I've removed him from The Farm (when his "remodelling" is finished!) I will be happy to work out another lease arrangement with you for a couple of months a year. I figure I'll get bored, if he's the only hometoy I have to play with all year long!

But that's enough about Tim. I'll have to stop for a "jackbreak" if I think about him any more just now!

I'm glad you could use the gay jailmeat I sent out. I'd like to pull the blonde milkpunk you kept, whenever he's ready. Let me do a "1-2-3-4" on him. He's a convicted rapist, you know. I'll enjoy squeezing his cream out four times in a row.

I'm sorry about the quick-squirter. Actually I think you should keep a couple of those babies, instead of sending them to The Cock and Ball as utility creamers. You could tie one up on a post at the tennis courts and we could take quick milk-guzzles between sets. Another good place for a fast-shooter would be next to the water fountain in the weight room.

I've found a guy (currently in the main holding cells, but soon to be transferred to the County Farm) with the monster foreskin your Lab freaks are looking for. He's got about a seven inch limp hang of thin meat, with what looks like three to four inches of loose skin below that. The only problem is that we're not sure he's open to gay sex, and he's an ugly brute! But then, if you're going to have a squash ball sewn into the pouch of your foreskin at the end of your dickhead, I guess looks aren't all that important. Shall I make further enquiries about his sexual tastes?

We'll have no trouble rounding up several young five-inch teats for you. I'll try to pick some gay street boys with nasty attitudes. I know how you like it if a new stud needs a little extra humiliation to turn him into the perfect milkpuppy. The "circumference pumping" sounds too weird even for me. Afraid I can't help you there.

Finally, I'm glad the three cops I recommended are going to become rookie members of The Farm. We'll come out as a foursome sometime. You are right about Jesse. The load he blew on that kid's face was outstanding. I've asked him to come to see me tomorrow for a "private" conference. I've got to get me some of that copcream too! I'll feel him out (while I'm feeling him up!) about doing "special duty" as a studcow once a month. Hell, if he's really good, I'll transfer him to The Farm as permanent "Dairy Liaison Officer" for rural affairs! Your suggestion for a weekend visit is definitely a "go." We'll have a good session with my nephew. There's enough meat there for both of us to chew on and enough milk to feed a family of four! And I'll bring some special

equipment for our "Interrogation" session with the media-stud.
I've got a vibrating mouthplug that gets a guy's throat so numb
you can stuff a fist down it! Keep it hard 'til Friday, Buddy,

The Chief

* * *

OUTGOING E-MAIL FILE
   Manager, The Milk Farm
TO:CEOPleaseCorp@LastResort.priv.
FROM:MGRJack@MFarm.priv.
[Encrypted message]
Sir:
I've just spent a weekend here at The Farm with the Chief and
we've examined the problem of Clay Brock, the reporter, *in depth*!
After a lot of hard pressing and considerable probing, Brock has
agreed to deliver to us, at the end of this coming June, his former
wife's son on his graduation from school. He has further agreed
that we should try to recruit the boy as security for Brock's continued silence. We have given him a membership to The Farm so
that we can tie him more closely to us in the meantime.

I think we can get enough video footage on Brock pulling on the
manteats in The Milking Barn to insure his loyalty and to guarantee that in a few months' time we'll be having a fresh eighteen-year-
old addition to the milking stock. Our highest priority now is to
ascertain that the boy is gay-inclined and to get some pictures of
his sex equipment.

We hope to see you soon. Isn't it about time for your semi-
annual visit to us? I've got a special boycow named Honeyboy—
the chief's nephew, in fact—that you'll like the taste of!

Hope you are enjoying The Last Resort.

All the best,
Jack

[Further File references: see Honeyboy//ThroatCondition
Results: Honeyboy//Swiss lease agreement: Teddy//School
locker room photos showing teat and milkbag size: Lab//Specifi-
cations for Precum Gel Capsules ("Honeypops"): Lab//Test
results of Vibrating Mouthgag (negative): Chief//Video of Brock
"interrogation".]

THE MILK FARM
MEMBERS' HANDBOOK

Hotel Reservations

The Milk Farm Hotel has only 30 rooms for single or double occupancy and The Milking Barn has a capacity limit of 60 members on any single day. It is, therefore, essential that members make reservations well in advance of their visits to The Farm, especially if they are bringing a guest who has not previously been approved by Security. Check-in time is 11:00 a.m.; check-out time is 10:00 a.m. Members must present their identity disks to the guard at the main gate. Taxis are not allowed on the grounds, but a car will be sent from the Hotel to pick up passengers at the gate who arrive by taxi. Limousines are allowed onto the grounds so long as the chauffeurs have been previously vetted by Security. Guests' chauffeurs and other servants may be accommodated in the guards' barracks and will be given access to some of the services of the Hotel, but will not be allowed into The Milking Barn unless they are registered as formal guests of their employers and stay with them in a Hotel room.

CHAPTER TWO

Teddy Goes to the Farm

I was born on a New Year's Day, so I was always a little older than most of my friends in school since I didn't start kindergarten until I was six. Two days after my eighteenth birthday, during my last year of high school, my mom found a sex magazine I'd hidden in the secret compartment of my gym bag. Whoever called it a "secret" compartment didn't know anything about mothers. She said she was just looking for dirty socks and jockstraps to wash, so maybe she wasn't snooping, but I have my doubts.

The magazine was *Torso* and some of the pictures, especially the big closeup two-page spreads of cocks and balls, were spotted with cum stains where I'd jerked off on them. Mom wanted to know who had sold it to me. I was able to say truthfully that someone had given it to me, but that I didn't know his name. In fact the man who owned the corner grocery near my school had seen me sneaking a peek at it one day after classes. He came over and asked me if I was interested in that kind of magazine.

"No, thanks, I was just looking," I stammered.

He took it off the rack, rolled it up, and stuck it down inside my jacket. "Take it," he said, "my gift. And if you like it, I've got some better ones upstairs in my apartment. I could show them to you some day."

I never had the nerve to go back into that store again, although he used to come to the window to wave at me when I walked by. Fortunately my mom was too mad to ask me any more questions. She just said that she wasn't going to have a queer for a son and that she would have Clay punish me.

Clay Brock is sort of my stepdad, even though my mom and he never bothered to get married. My real dad walked out on us when I was three, and after that I had a series of "dads" and "uncles" who came and went until I was ten, when Mom met Clay. She was selling real estate and showed him a condo. He bought it and soon

after we moved in with him and lived there as a family until I was eighteen.

When Clay came home that night from the offices of the publishing company where he was an investigative reporter for their magazines, I could hear from my bedroom my mom yelling at him.

"Look at this filth," she screamed. "You've got to take care of this, because I don't even want to see him again."

Clay came up to my room with the magazine in his hand. He closed the door and came over to sit beside me on the bed. I was scared, but I couldn't imagine how I would be punished, because no one had ever laid a hand on me. Clay is a strong guy, well-built and dominating when he wants to be. He opened up the magazine to a double-page picture of a huge uncut dick and two hairy balls. You couldn't see anything else: just the guy's thighs and crotch hair. The cock was leaking a bead of juice and the foreskin was really thick and plump around the head. Clay asked me what the stains on the picture were. I said I might have spilled some milk on it.

"Yeah, sure, some *milk*," he sneered.

Then suddenly he pushed me back on the bed and swung his leg over my body so he was straddling me, looking down at my surprised face. He held the magazine inches from my eyes.

"Lick it," he snarled.

I tried to get up, but he slapped my face with the open magazine.

"Lick it, or tell me the truth."

"Okay, okay, it's not milk, it's cum," I admitted. "I jerked off on the page."

My face must have been burning red because I'd never talked about sex at all with Clay. I hadn't really talked about sex with anybody.

After I confessed about the cum stains, Clay put the magazine down on the bed beside us and literally sat down on my chest, still straddling me. He just rested there with a little smile on his lips, watching me. Then he reached back and pressed the palm of his hand on my crotch. I started to get hard under my jeans. He unzipped me and reached into my shorts, pulling out my cock, which was stiff now and beginning to leak a little. He dug out my balls, while his other hand went to my throat, as if he were going to choke me. I could see a long lump in his own trousers, right in

front of my face, and I felt heat radiating from his crotch. Still with that cruel little smile, he took a tight grip on my cock and milked it up and down, slowly, but firmly, about ten or twelve times. I thought I was going to shoot all over his hand. When I started to groan, he let go and grabbed my balls. He put a slow squeeze on them until I whimpered.

Then he took away the hand that had been pressing on my throat and picked up the magazine, rolling it up into a club. He backed off my chest and stood between my spread legs at the side of the bed. Gathering my prick and my nuts into a bunch by circling them around the base with his fist, he whacked on them hard, twice, with the rolled-up *Torso*.

I yelled, but he mashed the magazine against my lips, covering my mouth with it. He leaned down so his mouth was close to my ear, stuck out his tongue, and licked around the inside of it.

"Find some place better to hide these things," he growled, and walked out, after flinging the magazine down sharply on my crotch.

I laid there for about five minutes, too stunned to do anything. Then I began to jerk my dick and in seconds I shot the biggest load of my life—to that point, anyway.

*   *   *

For the next five months, the final months of my high school senior year, he never mentioned the incident again. Sometimes in the morning when I was in the shower, he would come in to shave. When I stepped out and started to dry off, he'd grab my cock in one hand and my nuts in the other and mash them until I broke into a sweat and hissed in pain. Then he'd let go and continue his shave as if nothing had happened.

After the "punishment" in my bedroom, I began to see Clay's face when I beat my meat over the pictures in the sex mags, and I started to have wet dreams about being held down and pulled off by rough, hard hands, while a moist tongue licked my ear.

Relations between my mom and Clay deteriorated quickly shortly after that. I guess they never had gotten along very well. She didn't like being a writer's "wife": there wasn't enough money and no glamor, and Clay was often away working up long articles for magazines. As an investigative reporter, he'd have to travel

to other cities and live almost undercover sometimes to research a story.

Finally, in March after my eighteenth birthday, Mom moved out to live with the owner of the real estate firm she worked for. She said I could live with her if I wanted to, but I could tell she didn't really want me.

After the dirty magazine affair she had seemed to lose interest in me: I found myself on my own a lot, and I began to live in my own private world of television, video games, and jerkoff magazines. I had no special friends at school. I wasn't interested in dating girls, and I didn't know how to talk with the guys when they started bragging about all the pussy they were getting from their girlfriends. Every year I had tried out for the swim team, but never quite made it. For exercise I ran every day and I worked out in the weight room once in a while.

I liked the idea of being on my own in Clay's condo, if he would let me stay there. At the time he had been away for a couple of weeks working on a story in Chicago. I talked with him on the phone after he got the news from my mother about her new "husband." He said that it was fine with him if I wanted to stay on and look after things for him.

During the following months, the last of my high school days, I began to really get into jerking my meat and walking around the place nude, imagining what I might do if there was another guy in the house with me. Clay was gone all that time, finishing off a big exposé about union corruption, but I never had other kids in for parties. I was too shy to ask anyone over, even though most guys my age, with the free run of the house, would have had beer bashes every weekend. I still hadn't had sex with another guy. I just fantasized about it.

About a month before my graduation in late June, Clay started telling me, in our weekly phone calls, that he had something really special planned to celebrate the big event. He got home about a week before Graduation Day. For the first time I was alone in the condo with him. I thought maybe my dick and my nuts might get a little extra bathroom workout from him, now that we didn't even have to close the door when we were in there, but nothing happened. He just kept saying that on the weekend after Graduation, which fell on a Thursday, he was going to open up my world and

make me a different person. This sounded exciting and scary at the same time.

When the morning after a very boring Graduation Ceremony and an equally boring graduation party finally arrived, Clay told me to pack a small bag with clothes for three days. We were going to a special "resort."

*   *   *

We drove out of the city for about an hour and a half, not talking much. My few questions were answered with a curt "Just wait and see, Teddy." We came to a turning off the highway marked by a simple sign THE MILK FARM. I couldn't imagine why a visit to a dairy farm was supposed to be such a great graduation present!

Clay turned onto this road and drove about half a mile further until we came to a white rail fence with a gate and a small guardhouse. A guy in jeans and a work shirt came out and took a disk that Clay handed him. He checked with someone over his phone and waved us through. We drove another mile or so along a curving tree-lined drive until we came to a big, white, two-story house with a long porch across the front supported by massive square columns. The windows were framed by red shutters and the whole place looked impressive but friendly. Off to the left there was a large red barn and some other buildings. We pulled into a gravelled parking area off to the side of the house. There were fifteen or twenty other cars, mostly expensive foreign models and sports cars, and one black limo. We carried our two bags up to the open double doors of the house.

Inside there was a reception desk with a good looking guy behind it. Off to one side was a door to a bar, and there was a staircase up to the second floor. While Clay was checking in, I looked into the bar: I saw some men in shorts and T-shirts, and others in short terrycloth robes. A boy about my age came up to take our cases. He was barefoot and wore a T-shirt that said "Room Boy" on it, front and back. His white cotton shorts were so tight that they barely concealed the beefy cock stuffed into them, although his body was slim and undeveloped otherwise.

Our room faced the back of the house, and from our private balcony I could see a swimming pool and some tennis courts. There

were two other wings in a U-shape around the pool, making the building much larger than it seemed from the front. The room itself was spacious and comfortably furnished, with a big TV set and video recorder, two easy chairs, a mini-bar, and, I especially noticed, just one big bed for the two of us. There were leather cuffs attached to ropes hanging from the mattress at each corner of the bed, and I saw on the ceiling at its foot some big hooks and a pulley screwed into the wooden beams. Before I could begin to wonder about this, the Room Boy spoke.

"Will that be all, Sir?" He had a flirty air, teasing and sexy in a bratty way, even though that sausage in his shorts said that he was old enough to know exactly what he was doing.

Clay hooked his finger through the red strap around the boy's neck and pulled him roughly forward.

"No. Open my pants and take out my meat," he ordered.

As calmly as if this were part of his normal routine, the boy unzipped Clay's trousers. He reached in and pulled out Clay's semi-hard penis, tugging at it to make it bigger. Clay pushed him down to his knees, facing the rising dick.

"Now open your mouth, and show me what that red strap around your neck means, kid."

My own mouth dropped open as well, as the cute boy tilted his head back, opened his lips wide and stuck out a long pink tongue. Clay let his cock dangle, just barely skimming the wet surface, then dragged it over the boy's cheeks, leaving a slimy trail across that button nose. He looked over at me with a smile.

"Come over here, Teddy, and watch this closely."

I moved about three steps nearer, my hands in front of my crotch, hiding the huge boner that had sprung up in my jeans.

"I said get over *here*," he snarled. "Get down on your knees and put your face an inch from this suckpuppy's tongue on my dick."

I moved closer, knelt down, and slowly moved my head into a close-up side view of Clay's meat on that moist licker.

"Okay, sweetface, suck it. Show this baby here what a boy-mouth is for."

The guy started to move his tongue in circles over the head of Clay's cut dick, which began to swell even larger and to jerk up and down as the pink tongue did its job. I could smell the sex odor of precum leaking onto the boy's lips. He sucked the tip the way

he might suck his thumb. His wide, candid eyes took on a teasing, quizzical look, as if to say "Is this what I am supposed to do, Sir?"

Then Clay put his hand on the back of the kid's head, grabbing a fistful of the boy's soft bronze hair, and just jammed his whole long pole into his face. The Room Boy gave one gagging heave, then seemed to adjust to the invasion. His whole mouth just relaxed and his head fell even further back. His eyes locked avidly onto Clay's and stayed there while he used his throat to work the dickhead. His innocent expression changed into a look of raw desire.

It didn't take long before Clay began to moan: the kid's throat seemed to be massaging his cock somehow. Suddenly he pulled out, grabbed his bulging meat in one hand, and twisted the kid's bronze hair in the other. He shot a wet load of thick white jam right onto the boy's tongue which had followed the fat head instinctively knowing what was to come. The cumsucker didn't swallow. He just let the jism pile up in his mouth, spilling over onto his teeth and lips, and down his chin.

When the spurts died down a little, Clay took the glowing crown of his dick, dipped it into the brimming mouth, and spread the sticky sperm all over the boy's face, painting it with cum so it shined. My eyes were glued to that cockhead, smearing cum on the kid's cheeks, up into his nostrils, onto his earlobes.

Clay looked at me. "Put your hands behind your back," he commanded sharply.

I moved my hands from my crotch and clasped them in the small of my back. He could see that my fly was strained with a hard lump. I was just about ready to pop my own nuts.

"What have you learned, Teddy?" he asked.

I faltered, "What do you . . . I don't know what you mean . . . I . . ."

"That's the wrong answer, Teddy," he broke in. "That answer gets you no graduation presents. That answer just leaves you with a hard, frustrated teen cock leaking lube into your shorts. Get up," he said disgustedly, "and start unpacking."

I moved to the suitcases, still intensely aware that Clay's semi-hard cock was being continuously rubbed all over the Room Boy's smiling face. Finally Clay stuffed his dick back into his trousers.

"That's good, slutboy. Just put the suckcharge on my bill."

The guy got up, his mug white and shiny with cum. He licked his lips and smiled knowingly.

"Thank you, Sir, and if there's anything else I can do"—he looked directly at me—"please be sure to call. My name's Greg."

"I may just do that," Clay answered.

"Well, have a good session in The Milking Barn this afternoon," he smirked as he left, Clay's semen starting to dry a chalky white on his cheeks.

Clay turned to me. "I know you've got some questions and you're wondering just what goes on here, but I'm not going to tell you. I think it's a better surprise if you just experience this place without knowing everything in advance. It'll be more like opening a lot of graduation presents that way."

"Sure," I agreed, trying to get back in his good graces, "that's fine with me. I just hope next time you ask me what I've learned, I'll be able to give the right answers."

He laughed. "Don't worry about that, Teddy. This afternoon I've arranged for your lessons to be very clear and very thorough. And tonight I'll give you a complete test right here on this bed. If you don't pass the first time, I'll just keep giving it to you until you do. This is going to be more educational than any school course you've ever had."

I still had a woody from watching the Room Boy get plastered with Clay's cum, so I went into the bathroom, because I wanted to jerk off. Clay was hanging up his stuff in the closet. I had just sat down on the toilet seat and pulled out my throbbing dick and my heavy balls, when the door opened and Clay came in without warning. In his hand he had a six-inch leather paddle, about a quarter of an inch thick and an inch wide. It snapped with a sharp pop when he hit it across his palm.

"Get up and get your hands behind you," he ordered.

I stood up and braced my chest by clasping hands at the small of my back. My dick and balls hung out, swollen and as red as my face. He took my cock in his hand. It was like those times at home when he had manhandled my meat in the bathroom, but now he had this wicked looking little paddle. He cupped my cock in his palm and began to tap the length of it with the leather. The taps got harder and faster, and I started to breathe heavily. Then

he circled the top of my ball sack with his thumb and forefinger and pulled the quivering nuts forward and away from my crotch, squeezing them tight. He tapped the shiny nut sack with the paddle until I began to grunt. Releasing my balls, he went back to the shaft of my dick and gripped hard, so just the big purple head bulged out of his fist. He whacked the lips of my cockhole hard about ten times. Tears started to stream down my cheeks. I was still hard and horny, but somehow I knew I wasn't going to get any relief.

All this happened in silence except for my panting and whining and except for the snapping of the leather on my tender flesh. I never once thought to resist. I just took it, almost as if I wanted it. That's the way it had been since that first session with the sex magazine a year and a half ago. And he never seemed to imagine that I would resist either. He would just press, and mash, and pull my equipment as he pleased, but never for long, and he never let me cum. Then I would take care of myself after he left. Now, though, something new had been added—the paddle—and this time he didn't leave me to finish off.

"From now on you cum when you are allowed to cum, and eventually you will learn to cum when you are told to cum. From this moment, none of your good teensperm gets wasted. You'll see why later. Just tuck your meat back into your pants and come down with me to lunch. Don't worry about your hard-on. You'll see plenty of bulging packages while you're here. It's part of the fun."

He started to turn away, then looked back.

"Oh," he said, "you might as well get acquainted with this little pal." He held the black leather tormentor up to my lips. "Give it a kiss. You'll get to be good friends."

I pressed my lips to the leather.

"That's a good boy," he crooned. "Stick out your tongue and lick it up and down. Get it good and wet. Get to know it."

Something excited me about mouthing this piece of leather which had just been torturing my dick and slapping my balls. My saliva started to flow and I slobbered up and down the six inches until it was coated with spit, just like the Room Boy's face had been coated with Clay's jism.

Suddenly he jerked it away from my lapping caresses and rubbed

the wet surface back and forth across my sensitive cocklips, until they swelled up and I thought I would pass out. Then, abruptly, he walked out of the bathroom, but left the door open so he could make sure I didn't bring myself off, against his orders.

I stuffed my rod, still red, and slimy with spit and precum, back into my jeans and we went down to lunch with me looking like I had a baloney and two potatoes jammed down my crotch.

At lunch we sat at a table by ourselves because Clay said he didn't want the afternoon surprises to be spoiled by hearing other guys talk. While we ate our club sandwiches, he told me how he had first visited The Milk Farm on an assignment, but that, for various reasons, he'd never written the story. I learned later just what those "various reasons" were. He also talked about how he first began to be interested in men instead of women, a couple of years after he started living with Mom and me, and how he had always kept it a secret from everyone, except the anonymous tricks he picked up for sex. He asked me if I had ever had sex with a man, and I had to blush and say, "No, I just think about it a lot."

I guess it seemed a little weird how he could move so easily from one role to another. Sometimes he was just a normal father type, telling you what to do and talking about school and sports and his career. Then he would be a buddy, sharing sex experiences with you. And, of course, he was also the dominating master who squeezed your dick, told you not to cum, and fucked a boy's mouth while forcing you to watch. Somehow none of this bothered me. I was so excited and horny, and so curious, that I just accepted it all, as if it were the most normal thing in the world.

After lunch we went back to the room and Clay told me to take off my clothes and put on a terrycloth robe that was hanging in the closet. These robes were just long enough to cover your cock and balls. He did the same, and we both slipped on some light sandals that were on the floor of the closet. My cock had gone down a little, so my robe didn't tent out in front of me too much.

We walked down the stairs, joining other men as they headed out of the Hotel and toward the big red building with the sign on it saying MILKING BARN. Inside the glass double doors at one end of the barn, we entered a kind of lobby with chairs and plants and a place to hang our robes if we wanted to. Some guys took off their robes and went on through the next set of doors nude.

Others had jockstraps or briefs on; some were in light trousers or jeans with only their shirts off, and some went in fully clothed.

I wanted to keep my robe on, but Clay took it off me and hung it up on a hook with his own. Just then a rugged looking guy dressed in white trousers and a tight white T-shirt came up to us. On his shirt were the words MILK MASTER. Clay seemed to know him.

"Teddy, this is the Milk Master for today. You don't need to know his name, you just call him 'Sir.' He's going to take you into the milking room and give you your first lessons."

"Hi, Teddy." He held out his hand and I shook it. Then he reached down and felt my dick and my balls. "You're a good looking young stud, Teddy. It'll be a pleasure to teach you the ropes here in The Milking Barn." Then he put his arm around my shoulder and walked me through the double doors with Clay following behind.

Inside, I got the surprise of my life, a surprise that's still going on!

THE MILK FARM
MEMBERS' HANDBOOK

The Milking Barn

The Milking Barn is open daily from 2:00 p.m. to 6:00 p.m. and again from 9:00 p.m. to midnight. During those hours members have unlimited access to the pleasure stock on view in the stalls. The only exceptions are certain specialized services which must be reserved in advance at the main desk of the Hotel and for which there will be extra fees.

The attendants in the Barn are there to assist members upon request and to bring fresh stock into the stalls. The word of the Milk Master is law in the Barn and no member may appeal any of his decisions about the use of the stock.

A refreshment bar will be found at the far end of the center aisle.

CHAPTER THREE

Teddy's First Pull

The main room of The Milking Barn was big—long, with a high peaked ceiling, just like a real barn. Down a wide center aisle there were comfortable looking sofas and easy chairs in groups facing either direction into the stalls which ran down the sides. These boxes were like double horse stalls, about twelve feet wide, and looked to be about twelve feet deep. The lighting was dim except for bright pinspots which shone down into the stalls, making them glow and look like little stage sets with the chairs and sofas facing into them like seats in a theatre. I couldn't see what was in the stalls yet, but I could see some of The Milk Farm clients walking up and down the center aisle looking into the lighted boxes, sometimes entering, out of my sight. Others were sitting in the lounge areas watching what was going on in the stalls.

"Teddy, The Milk Farm is just what its name says," explained the Milk Master. "It's a resort where guys go to drink milk. The only thing different is that our milk is manmilk and our cows are mancows. And the customers get to drink their fill, right from the source, right from the big manteats themselves."

I looked in wonder at Clay, who grinned. "That's right, Teddy. You're going to have a very milky eighteenth graduation party!"

The Milk Master came up behind me and pressed his body against mine. He reached around and began to rub my nipples with his thumbs. I could feel the hard lump in his crotch nudging my ass cheeks.

"You are about to have an experience few young men ever get," he breathed in my ear, "because membership in The Milk Farm resort is a very expensive proposition. So it's usually middle-aged, well-off guys who come here. But we also like to have young clients as well." One hand moved down and fondled the head of my dick. "We encourage members like your stepdad, Mr. B. here, to bring along college boys and younger guys. It makes the whole scene more stimulating for everybody."

I was to learn later just what kind of "encouragement" they had given Clay to get him to bring me to The Milk Farm.

The Milk Master put his hand on the back of my neck and gently propelled me toward the first stall on the left. As we came up to it, I saw a sign on a stand at the front:

STALL A
Pure Whole Milk
Station 1   Sweetheart
Station 2   Rusty
Station 3   Protein Bill

Inside the stall, on each of the three walls there was a guy attached to the wood panelling. Each one had leather cuffs on his neck, wrists, and ankles. The cuffs were attached to chains about six inches long which were screwed into the walls, allowing his body to move a little bit. His arms and legs were spread widely against the dark, polished panelling and there was a kind of a rail sticking out from the wall ass-high, which caused his crotch to thrust forward. Each man's dick arched out in a semi-swollen state and they all had nice, hanging balls.

While I stared, my mouth open, my dick rearing up in excitement at the sight, another client came into the stall and walked up to the mancow at Station 1, the one named "Sweetheart" on the sign. He knelt down and began to pull at the cow's meat with long slow sucking movements.

The Milk Master lightly stroked my ass cheeks as he explained the set-up. "Teddy, most of the stalls have three studcows strapped into them. The milkstock in each stall has special qualities. These dicks, for example, give a good, solid flow of whole, rich manmilk. Their sexcream is sweet and fresh and has a natural flavor. They are trained to give a big portion, maybe about a third of a cupful of warm ballmilk, but they don't gush, like some other of our specialty manteats. These are the dependable, steady spurters, just the right sort of cow for your first pull."

"Pull, Sir?" I asked, completely dumbfounded by the images that began to form in my mind.

"That means that this will be the first spermtit you suck the milk out of," he explained. "Later you'll pull other kinds of milk and learn other milking techniques, but for now we'll start off with the basics."

He reached down and slowly pulled my dick, squeezing it like a farmer milking a real teat. "I don't have to ask you if that's okay because I can see from your own milkdick that you're ready to drink some fresh manjuice."

The stud named Sweetheart began to breathe heavily and his body started jerking against the straps. His milker was pulling on his fat teat with his lips locked firmly around the big head.

"You can see, Teddy, that Sweetheart is about to feed his milker. When his sexmilk actually shoots into the sucker's mouth, he may moan, like a cow in heat. We don't let any of the stock speak when they're in the stalls and in service, but they are allowed to make certain sounds that tell the customer how they're feeling."

Clay had been standing in front of the cow named Protein Bill, fingering the guy's heavy balls and rubbing his thumb against his cumhole. He put his hand up to his mouth and licked at the glistening precum on it. "This cowjock has a really sweet taste. Maybe we should start Teddy off with him," he suggested.

The Milk Master disagreed, "I think his teat may be a little big for a beginner. I had Rusty in mind for Teddy's first lesson. What do you think, Mr. B.?"

"Sure, I guess you're right," allowed Clay. "Let's not scare him off on his first suck."

I looked at Rusty. He was at Station 2, on the back wall. Rusty seemed younger than me. He had a mischievous Tom Sawyer look with his uncombed carrot-top and his shining green eyes in a freckled face. His skin was creamy, with just a light dusting of ginger colored hair from his "outie" belly button to the thatch at his crotch. He had a neat, compact body with small pecs and little brown button nipples, but his cock was man-sized without being scary: about six inches, and plump and juicy looking with a white shaft and a red cockhead to match his hair. I learned later that all the cowteats and milkbags got a lot of special treatment to give them that succulent appearance.

The Milk Master watched me devouring the boycow with my eyes. "I think Rusty's just the thing for you, Teddy—a nice, friendly little package of boyteat and cumballs ready to shoot their milk for you."

Rusty grinned when he heard this, his crooked teeth giving him a dopey, innocent expression, but I didn't have much time to look

at it, because the Milk Master and Clay took my arms and quickly had me on my knees facing Rusty's sturdy dick.

The Milk Master took the meat lightly in his fingers and held it up for me to look at. "You've never had a cock in your face before, have you Teddy?"

"No, Sir, I haven't," I confessed.

"Have you ever tasted your own cream off your fingers when you milked yourself?"

"No, Sir, never." I don't know why I was ashamed to admit that I'd never eaten my own cum!

"Good," said the Milk Master, "I like to train a virgin milker." He looked at Clay. "Mr. B., maybe you'd like to go over and get some of Protein Bill's dickmilk while I give Teddy his first lesson. I think it's best if this is just between him and me."

"That's fine with me. I know he's in good hands," said Clay as he moved off out of my line of sight.

The Milk Master began my instruction. "Now Teddy, Rusty is here for one purpose, and one purpose only. He's here to produce milk for you to drink. All you have to do is pull it out of him. The pulling is all the fun and the milk is the reward for that fun." He squeezed Rusty's prong a little harder and put his hand on my back so that I inched forward on my knees toward it. "This teat is just right for a beginning milker like you. It's not so long that you'll have to worry about gagging, but it's thick enough to fill your mouth and give your tongue and your cheeks something to work on."

By now Rusty's prick was inches from my lips.

"Just lean forward, Teddy, and open your mouth," the Master instructed. "No, don't close your eyes. Learn to keep your eyes open. You want to see what you're sucking. . . . That's it. . . . You don't have to open your mouth that wide yet. Just let it hang open naturally."

I was so hot, I felt like I wanted to lunge onto the dick and swallow it whole. But I held back and tried to follow the Milk Master's direction. He put his hand on my jaw and worked it around until it was loose; then he put two fingers in my mouth and told me to relax as he explored my oral cavity with his musky tasting probes. My mouth started to water. He said that was great, that the best milkers always had wet, sloppy mouths, and that the cows

like a wet suck.

Then, pinching my cheeks to keep my mouth open, he brought the head of Rusty's red teat just to my lips and moved it around on them slowly.

"Now, Teddy, I want you to get your tongue out—just a little —don't try to do too much. Just let me see the tip of it. . . . That's right. Now I'm just going to rub the tip of your tongue with his hot cockhead.

I felt a warm softness. There was a tart taste to it, a little like a sour lemon drop melting on my tongue.

The Milk Master kept up his soft instructions in my ear. "Now, Teddy, I want you to move just the tip of your tongue around the very end of this milkhead. Can you feel those two little bumps, those two little milklips?" I nodded my head, not wanting to move off that mouthwatering spot. "That's where Rusty's pure, whole milk is going to come from. You've got to learn to work those little milklips with your tongue tip. Brush it back and forth across them. Lap at those swollen little lips like a cat lapping at its milk."

Rusty made a kind of sighing sound in his throat.

The Master praised me. "That's good, Teddy. Did you hear your cow pant? He likes that. He wants to feed you, Teddy. He wants you to drink all his milk."

I started flicking the lips of Rusty's milkdick harder, trying to make him pant and groan some more. I put my hand on my own hard prick to jerk it.

"No, Teddy," the Milk Master's voice was sharp. "You are here to suck and to drink. Your own milk will be taken later. I don't want to have to tell you again."

"Yes, Sir," I apologized, "I'm sorry, Sir."

"Besides," he continued firmly, "I think you should start using your hands on Rusty's equipment. Put your right hand up under his milkbags and just hold them lightly—no squeezing—Rusty doesn't need that kind of rough milking to produce a load for you."

I cupped Rusty's two boynuts in their soft sack, feeling the fuzz on them. They quivered when I tightened my fingers around them.

"Put your other hand on his teat and grasp it gently. Just press on it a little and pull it a bit as you work the tip of his milkhead with your tongue."

I felt as though I hadn't even been alive until this moment.

Kneeling in front of a red-haired boy, fondling his balls, fingering his shaft, tonguing his cockhead—it was like the beginning of the world for me.

The Milk Master took me further into my new universe. "Now let's start working on the whole head, Teddy. Move your tongue in a big circle all over that big fat milkcrown. Feel that ridge running around it? Feel the meeting spot underneath? That's called the frenulum. Lick that triangle beneath the head where the lines of the ridge meet. Service every inch of that cow's meat, Teddy. The better you serve him the more milk you'll get."

I lapped my tongue on the loose skin just beneath his dickhead, tickling the spot until Rusty squealed and tried to thrust his teat deeper into my mouth.

The Milk Master was ready with the next step. "Now, I want you to open your mouth wide. Let that milkdick slide forward on your tongue until your lips just pass the ridge of the crown. Lock your lips hard around that ledge, and work your whole tongue on that milkbulb at the same time. Feel how your cow's trying to force the pace by pushing deeper? But you've got to keep in control. Give him a little chomp down with your teeth if you have to, just to let him know who's in charge. . . . That's right. Hear him hiss? He'll stop trying to rush you now. Gradually work your lips up the shaft. . . . Keep your tongue moving. . . . Don't close your eyes. . . . Keep going, Teddy, keep going till that little mouth of his cumhole hits the back of your throat."

I felt the whole length of Rusty's milkmeat moving into my mouth until the heat of the cockhead warmed my tonsils. When I started to gag, the Master made me stop and just hold the long tube quietly in my mouth while he whispered in my ear, telling me what a good milker I was going to be and how the cows would all want to give me their biggest loads of cream.

My lesson in "basic" milksucking went on for about an hour. When my lips got tired and I started to pull away, the Milk Master would put his hands on my jaw and on my throat and massage them until I relaxed again. Not once did I get to take the milkteat out of my mouth. I learned to keep at it. "The milk is the thing," said the Master, "and you can't get the milk if you don't suck the teat."

I learned to hollow my cheeks so their soft inner lining caressed

the shaft; I learned to thrust my whole throat down onto the milk-stick until my nose was buried in Rusty's wiry red cockhair; I learned to manipulate the milkballs subtly and to feel the mancow start to tighten up before shooting; I learned how to pull back so the cow wouldn't squirt, without actually losing touch with the teat, so that I could bring him in ever-increasing excitement toward a big milkspurt. And finally, when I thought my mouth would freeze into its open position and when Rusty was making a con-tinuous whine of frustration from being denied his climax so long, the Milk Master said, "Ok, Teddy, you've earned it. Suck that baby dry."

—my first mancum, splashing against the roof of my mouth, coating my tongue, spurting against the back of my throat, slosh-ing in my cheeks, a big mouthful of warm, white, pure manmilk—

It tasted so good I began to pull and suck at that teat again, try-ing to get another load immediately. But the Milk Master pulled me off, laughing, "You'll do, Teddy. You've got all the right in-stincts, but you've got to learn when to let the teat go. Rusty has to be taken back to the stock lounge to rest now. Each cow is con-ditioned to give at least four basic loads a day with a minimum half-hour rest between each pull. And in the meantime we'll bring in a fresh cow and strap him into this station." He pulled me up to my feet. By now Clay was also back at my side. They both wiped some milk from my chin and neck and held out their hands for me to lick. I leaned down and slurped at their fingers eagerly. Then, realizing what I was doing, I drew back, embarrassed.

"Don't be ashamed of wanting every drop you can get," Clay said. "That's the sign of a true connoisseur."

※　※　※

We walked into the main aisle. "Let's sit down for a while and watch some of the action," suggested the Milk Master, "—get you better acquainted with the place." We passed a couple of stalls: one was labelled:

STALL C
Heavy Creamers
Station 1   Thick Jim
Station 2   Custard Boy
Station 3   Chocolate Syrup

The Master explained, "This stall is for cows who give an especially rich and creamy load, Teddy. These big teats produce a studcream so thick that it just oozes out like pudding, and the milker licks it off the cumlips, letting it coat his whole tongue and the inside of his mouth."

Clay reached down and took my swollen dick in his fist, pulling on it while the Master talked.

"These creamcows have had milk-enhancement hormones," he continued, "and can produce about a half a cup of nectar at every milking."

This talk was getting me so horny, I started to thrust my prick back and forth in Clay's slow-moving fist. The Milk Master looked down at my crotch. "Bad boy, Teddy," he warned, "you're trying to cum after I warned you not to. We'll have to teach him a little lesson, won't we, Mr. B.?"

Clay nodded and squeezed the shaft of my cock so hard I thought it would collapse: the head inflated and got a deep red. The Master bent down and opened his mouth over the end of my engorged cockhead. He put his teeth right on the cocklips which were now pouty and dribbling precum. He bit down sharply and ground his front teeth back and forth on the cocktip until I forgot all about wanting to cum and just wanted him to stop chewing on me.

"Please don't," I whimpered, "I won't try to cum, I promise."

But he didn't quit right away. He moved those grinding teeth up further onto the sensitive head of my prick and chewed the glans lazily, like a dog chewing on a bone that's all used up. Clay leaned in and nipped at my earlobe, spreading the pain around in my body until I begged them to stop.

Finally the Milk Master straightened up from my shuddering crotch. "If I catch you trying to shoot your milk again, without permission, I'll make permanent bite marks on your penis, and that would be a pity because we've got some exciting future plans for that pretty piece of teenmeat, don't we, Mr. B.?"

"Yes," said Clay, "just be patient, Teddy. You'll get to shoot your load, I promise you."

Next to the Heavy Creamers stall was a smaller box, about half the size of the regular ones. A sign said:

STALL D-One
Specialty Cow
Gusher

In it there was a single studcow, but he was tied to a pole in the center of the space instead of being strapped to one of the walls. He was a muscular football-player type—sandy hair, pug-nose, big pecs and thighs, and a thick milkdick about five inches long with enormous balls the size of oranges drawn up below. His wrists were tied together and hooked higher above his head to the stanchion pole, and his ankles were strapped together against the pole about three feet above the floor. Every six inches his body was tightly strapped to the steel pillar so he couldn't move at all. His fat milkteat was just mouth-high to the man who stood in front of him, ready to milk him.

"It looks like Gusher is going to get popped," chuckled the Milk Master. "Let's stop here and watch this guy take his cream."

We sat on a deep, comfortable sofa, facing toward the brightly lighted stall, me in the middle, the Milk Master and Clay on either side. The Master had one arm around my shoulders; he reached down with his other arm and brought my hand into his bulging crotch. He opened his white pants and pulled out a long piece of warm meat which he wrapped my hand around, letting me know that he wanted me to fondle him. Then he reached for my own teat and slowly squeezed and pulled at it while we watched. Clay reached under my dick and played with my nuts, rolling them between his fingertips and tugging at the little hairs on my ballsack. But he slapped my hand away when I tried to handle his cock the way I was caressing the Master's.

"The Gusher is a very special type of creamcow," explained the Master. "He doesn't ooze his cream, he spews it out. His rich cum just gushes out that hole, and it's been known to measure over a cup if the milker has held him off long enough."

We watched as the man began his service at the Gusher's teat. Because he was standing, he could get his whole body into his pulling, drawing at the thick tube like he was playing a game of tug-o-war with the cow's meatrope. After a while the muscular jock began straining at his straps, trying to thrash around, while the milker sucked him with a fevered intensity and pressed both hands at the base of the Gusher's pulsing dick and balls, tightening the

whole package into a mound of throbbing flesh.

Then the Gusher started to bellow like a bull, and he tried to thrust his meat as far forward as he could into the milker's face. His muscles spasmed and rippled and his bellow became one long roar. There were wet sounds coming from the sucker's mouth and he moaned and hummed in pleasure as the cow fed him. We saw his throat swallowing frantically, and then big gobs of creamy white syrup started spilling out of his lips around the thick teat. The Gusher's creamtube just kept pulsing and shaking in the milker's mouth. He brought his hands up to his chin and tried to catch the flow, so as not to waste it. It slopped over his cupped hands and ran down his arms.

The bull-bellowing, and the wet humming, and the gushing overflow went on for what seemed like five or ten minutes, until the Gusher suddenly slumped back on the pole, as if he had lost consciousness. The milker didn't back off, though. He kept at the bullteat, working it with his slick mouth and his slimy hands, rubbing his face over the whole area, until the cow's groin and thighs were covered with sperm and saliva. Then he licked every surface that had a drop of that good rich cream on it, until there wasn't a speck left on the cow's body. When he finally got up, his face was red and shiny, and he had a thin coat of jism all over it. He was smiling dreamily, as if he had just won the lottery.

As he moved out of the stall toward us, the Milk Master spoke to him. "Well, Mr. M., it looks like you rang the Gusher's bell good today."

"Oh, yes," the man agreed happily, "He just about drowned me today."

"Listen, Mr. M.," the Master said, "this is a first-timer, young Teddy here, with his stepdad, Mr. B. I know he'd like to have a taste of Gusher's cream. How about letting him lick the last of it off your face?"

"My pleasure," he agreed eagerly; he knelt down in front of me so I could run my tongue up and down his cheeks and around his mouth, picking up the last succulent traces of the Gusher's load. It was like warm vanilla custard, so potent that I felt a little drunk just from those few licks. I don't know how Mr. M. could even walk after slugging down a cup of the stuff.

In the stall, two Milking Assistants took the Gusher down from

his post and carried him off through a small door at the back. The Milk Master told us that at the moment The Farm only had one cow who could gush his load in that way, so milking him was a "surcharge service" since he could only produce one load every two days. He said there was a waiting list of clients hoping to get a pull of that unique sperm.

* * *

After that, we walked around and looked into all the stalls on both sides of the aisle. The Master kept up a running description of the types of cows available and we saw a lot of guys pulling all kinds of milk from all kinds of teats. The gasps and moans and groans and bellows of the studcows as their milk was siphoned off made the whole place even sexier. And the gobbling and swallowing sounds of the drinkers added to the horny atmosphere. At a stall labelled NEW STOCK we were watching a distinguished looking black guy stuff an ivory-skinned kid's prick and balls in his mouth, all at the same time, when one of the Milking Assistants approached. He waited until the Milk Master beckoned him over.

"Master," he reported, "a customer has pulled Big Mack over in the Light Creamers Stall three times in a row and wants to reserve him for another pull this afternoon and then take him into the 5-6-7 Room this evening."

"So, what's the problem?"

"Well, Big Mack said in the stock lounge during his last rest period that the guy is a really amateur sucker with a crude technique. He doesn't think he can shoot for the milker another four times today."

The Milk Master turned to us. "I'll have to go and see to this. Why don't you two just wander around. I'll be back very shortly."

"Sure, go ahead," Clay nodded. "We'll go down to the bar for a drink."

As we walked toward the small refreshment bar at the far end of the center aisle, I asked Clay what the 5-6-7 Room was.

"It's a special private suite near the stock lounge at the rear of the barn," he explained. "Each cow can be milked four times during a day, usually two or three times in the afternoon and maybe once during the evening session, but generally by different cus-

tomers. If a client decides he wants to use a cow all day, and if he thinks he can take the cow further than the standard four pulls, he applies for a '5-6-7 milking.' "

We came up to the bar and sat on high stools. Clay ordered a "draft with a head" for each of us. This turned out to be a light ale which the bartender topped off with a foamy layer of his own tart piss. While I sipped this drink, not sure whether I liked its bitter taste or not, I asked Clay if he had ever milked a stud seven times in one day.

"No, Teddy, I haven't. I hope to some day. In fact I've got my eye on a very special cow that I'd like to drain, but so far I haven't felt I had the skill or the money to do it. The 5-6-7 Room requires a surcharge fee in addition to the normal daily milking fees, and it's a hefty one."

While we were talking a slim dark-skinned guy with a small, uncut dick climbed up onto the bar between us and leaned back, spreading his legs wide. "I thought you might like some stuffed olives to nibble on," offered the bartender. "Oliver, here, is our 'olive boy.' Let me show you." He set a dish of jumbo pitted green olives on the bartop by Oliver's thigh. Picking one up he brought it down to the tip of the young man's slender prick and, with the fingers of his other hand, pulled on his foreskin so it came forward off the head of his meat. It was then we saw that his foreskin was very long and thin, and tender enough to be threaded through the big hole in the olive. When the bartender was finished stuffing the olive, the kid's dick had a big green juicy bulb on its end with his brown foreskin sticking out the top like a ruffle.

The bartender held the morsel up and smiled at me. "How about a nibble on this, Sir?" I must have looked very confused, because Clay laughed and said, "Just lean down and bite the olive off the end of his cock, Teddy. And be sure to give his skin a sharp nip when you do it."

Before long I got the hang of it. Clay would thread the long foreskin through an olive, and I would chew it off, causing the boy to wince and shiver. But he never closed his thighs and eventually his little cockhead got hard and filled out so much of the long foreskin that we had to stop. The bartender said we were welcome to suck out the boy's "olive oil" as well, if we wanted, but Clay said he thought that the beer was enough.

I told Clay I had to take a leak, after the "draft with a head," so we went into the toilet just off the bar. There were two urinals. One, the standard white porcelain pisser, and the other a man sitting against the tile wall with his neck strapped tight against it. He was blindfolded and his mouth was open. Above him a sign read "Piss Mouth." I moved toward the white porcelain urinal, too shy to use the human one, but Clay took my arm and moved me in front of the guy with his tongue hanging out. I had to wait a little while, because just looking at those wide open lips on a blindfolded face made my dick get hard again, but soon the pressure on my bladder was too great and I sank my semi-hard pisser in the man's mouth and heard him gurgle as I filled his throat. Then Clay watered him as well and we went back out into the Barn.

The Milk Master was waiting at the bar, having settled the matter of the client who wanted the 5-6-7 Room. He asked if I wanted to watch a stud getting milked to the outer limits of his capacity.

"Sure," I said enthusiastically, "that would be great."

The Master laughed and looked at Clay. "We've got a real keener here, haven't we, Mr. B.? How about it? Shall we go and take a peek in the 5-6-7 Room?"

"Yeah," Clay jumped at the chance, "I'd like to see just what goes on in there myself."

The 5-6-7 Room was just down a short hallway next to the bar. We went past the door with "5-6-7" on it to an unmarked door a few feet beyond. Inside was a small dark room with a long sofa facing a big window which looked into the dimly lighted Box.

"This is a one-way mirror," explained the Milk Master. "From here we can watch all the action without disturbing the fun the guys are having inside."

As we sat on the sofa, with me between the two of them, so they could play with my meat again and pinch my tits while we watched, I saw that one of the best looking of the studcows—a guy with shiny black hair and the sultry look of a gypsy—was leaning back against a Milking Assistant, while a man knelt before him and pulled rhythmically at his dark, streamlined teat. Then I realized that the Milking Assistant behind wasn't just supporting the studcow, he was fucking him! He jabbed the gypsy's ass with short quick strokes while another Assistant stood beside them pulling and twisting the stud's tits.

The Milk Master leaned closely toward my ear and began to explain the 5-6-7 experience in his husky voice as he gently squeezed my cock. "A customer of The Milk Farm can drink as many loads a day as he can manage, Teddy. But no cow can be pulled for more than four loads in succession without a minimum rest of a half an hour between each pull."

I remembered how Rusty, my first pull, had been led off after I had drained him.

"The only exception to the daily four-pull rule is the 5-6-7 Room," the Milk Master continued. "If a customer is having a really good session with a cow's teat, he can apply for a 5-6-7 extension. At that point I decide whether the stud and the customer are up to another three pulls. If I think the cow's got it in him and if the drinker seems to know what he's doing, they are both moved here to the 5-6-7 Suite with two Milk Assistants in attendance."

Clay chimed in, "Don't imagine that The Milk Farm offers this service for free, Teddy. Believe me, the extra charges for a 5-6-7 session are astronomical."

"Maybe, but I never heard a customer complain," countered the Milk Master, "and nobody ever asks for his money back!"

In the room the Milk Assistant began ramming his cock even more savagely into the stud's ass and the other Assistant pulled the guy's tits out a good inch from his pecs and rotated them fast and hard in his pinching fingers. The cow began to shudder and heave and the customer at his dick pressed his face firmly against the creamboy's crotch hair, letting the massive teat swell out his throat as it pumped out its fifth load of milk that day.

The Master looked on approvingly. "The fifth pull is usually not too difficult, as you can see. Sometimes we use a dildo vibrator to stimulate the cow's joy button, but the Milk Assistants like to get in a little fucking practice so usually we do it the 'natural' way."

In the room the two Assistants attached the studcow's neck, arms and legs tightly to the wall with leather straps; another leather belt was fastened snugly at his waist, so that he was immobilized against the wall with only his milkballs and creamtube hanging heavy and loose. The customer had leaned back on his thighs, savoring the taste of the last milkload, as he watched the big sperm nipple being readied for the next assault.

The Master put his hand behind my neck and pulled my face

down into his crotch. His dick and balls rested between his thighs, radiating heat against my mouth and cheek which he pressed down into the mound of warm flesh. "Lick my nuts for a little while, Teddy. There's not much to look at while they get started on the sixth pull."

I let my tongue wander over his big testicles as he continued his description of the 5-6-7 experience. "Load number six is usually a matter of talking the cum out of the stud's teat. The two Assistants stand on either side of the cow and go through a ritual of hypnotic questions and answers while the milker gently pulls with a soft mouth. But this time the sucker really has to coax the juice out."

"Why do they strap the stud down so tightly for this pull?" Clay asked.

"At this stage," answered the Master, "it's important for the cow to concentrate completely on his teat and his milkbags and on the cream that he's got to produce from them. Being tied down centers his attention on his cream spout. He's got to start thinking of himself as one big milktube from head to toe. That's what the question and answer routine does for him. Here, I'll turn on the room microphone so you can hear a bit of it." He pressed a button on the console next to the sofa and we heard a kind of chant from the room beyond the glass. I started to raise my head to look at the scene, but he pushed me firmly back into the warm Vee of his crotch. "Keep working those balls with that pink tongue of yours, Teddy. You can hear well enough down there. You don't have to look."

From the speakers I heard a litany repeated again and again over the sound of wet suckling noises.

"What are you?"
"I'm a studcow."
"What do you give?"
"I give manmilk."
"How much do you give?"
"All my milker wants."
"Where is your milk?"
"In my milkteat."
"Where is your milk?"
"In my milkbags."

"Where is your milk?"

"In my belly."

"Where is your milk?"

"In my chest."

On and on the questions and answers went until the cow's responses began to be little more than a half-spoken moaning. Finally there was a long, sighing cry and I heard greedy smacking and guzzling noises as the sucker drew a clean, clear flow into his throat. The mancow was letting go of every ounce of milk left in his body from his tits to his teat.

At last the Master let me sit back up so I could look at the scene in the 5-6-7 Room. The studcow hung limply from his straps while the milker covered every inch of his crotch with loving strokes of his milk-coated tongue. The Milking Assistants seemed to be stimulated by the sixth pull. Both of them had their cocks in their hands and were working them strongly, rubbing the sticky precum from their cockheads onto the stud's thighs. "I don't see how in hell that cow's going to give up another load," said Clay, shaking his head. "He looks to me like he's been milked dry."

"Oh, this guy's a good little milkbull. He'll go the distance," the Milk Master assured us. "Now it's up to the milker to show his stuff. The seventh pull is really a mystical kind of milking. Most seven-pull milkers have their private techniques for sucking out that last precious juice. This particular client has almost infinite patience. See, he's starting his routine now. He's taking long slow pulls with his lips from the base of the cow's teat to its tip. He'll do five hundred of those in the same slow sensuous movement." The Master took my hand in his and brought it down to his swelling meat. "Put your fist around my dick, Teddy, and give me a slow sexy handjob in time to the sucker's moves."

I began to move my hand up and down on his cock, pacing my pulls to the fascinating undulations of the milker's mouth on the studcow's teat. Before I knew it, the five hundred pulls were over, and the sucker moved his lips down to the milkbags hanging ripely between the stud's spread legs. He sucked both balls into his cheeks and slowly turned his head from side to side as far as he could stretch, pulling those big soft nuts in a rhythmic swinging arc.

"He'll do five hundred of those ball-pulls as well," the Master said, as he moved my hand, wet with his precum, down to his own

nuts, instructing me to squeeze them gently in time to the sucker's head swings from side to side. "After that he'll grasp the dick hard in his fist with just the big head swollen out, and he'll circle the dicklips right at the milkhole with just the tip of his tongue. He'll do five hundred revolutions each direction—clockwise and counter clockwise."

In the 5-6-7 Suite the exotic looking studcow's head was up and pressed against the wall; his dark hair, parted in the middle, fell in waves framing his high cheekbones. His eyes were half open, staring through their long lashes blankly into some middle distance and his full lips seemed to curve slightly up at the corners into a secret smile. He seemed to be in a semi-trance, floating up into some milky heaven.

Clay stood up suddenly, his cock stretching out stiff and throbbing before him, drooling a honey colored liquor in one long golden thread. "God, I can't watch this any more—I'm going to pop before I'm ready to. Let's get out of here," he pleaded.

"Okay," the Master agreed, "the seventh load isn't much to look at anyway. It can take many forms. Sometimes the seventh pull seems to tap some hidden reservoir finally and the milk that the cow's been unconsciously storing away just gushes out—as much as a cup of the sweetest nectar you can imagine. I've seen the milker literally get drunk on it and have to be helped back to the Hotel. But other times the seventh cum is almost protoplasmic. It's like milk that hasn't even come into being yet. The drinker knows it's coming because the cow starts to hyperventilate: when that happens the sucker gets a firm hold on the tube—not too tight—and lets the head of the teat hover just inside the ring of his open mouth. And out comes a fine sort of milky mist, a sweet spray that just hisses out, light as air but with an indefinable taste of spice."

These mental images were too much for Clay. He gasped and grabbed his dick tightly. "Damn it, you tricky bastard, I told you I couldn't take any more of this!" He stepped in front of me and thrust his meat into the Milk Master's face. "Eat my load, you fucker." The Master gave a shout of laughter and sank his mouth over Clay's spurting cock. I kept squeezing the Master's nuts and watched as the sucker behind the window moved to his hypnotic licking of the stud's swollen milklips. Clay stopped thrusting into the Master's throat, letting his wet meat slip from the Master's lips

and hang wetly against his thigh; we got up and moved toward the door.

"What happens to the milkstud after the seventh load?" I asked.

"He'll have to be carried back to the dormitory on a stretcher," the Master answered. "We'll put him in a dark room and let him sleep for at least 24 hours. When he comes back on line he'll have a different look to him. You can usually tell guys who've been through a 5-6-7 session. Their teats are fuller, riper somehow, and they'll kind of drift off when they're getting milked by a master sucker, as if they're remembering some wonderful day in a lost paradise."

As we came out into the hallway we saw a big man in work fatigues sweeping the floor toward the rear of the building. "You see that hunky guy over there, with that dreamy sort of expression on his face?" pointed out the Master. "He's one of our mistakes. We let a really greedy customer take him to eight pulls, then nine, and finally ten! After the tenth cum, he just sort of went away, mentally, and we're having to pull him back gradually. He's got a massive white milktube, but it just won't get hard anymore. We stick a low-level vibrator up his ass every night for eight hours while he sleeps, and I noticed this morning that his dick was a little firmer than it has been. We've arrived at the magic number seven as the maximum number of pulls allowed on any one cow through a certain amount of trial and error."

Clay could see that I was a little frightened by what the Master was saying. "Don't you think it's time we let this guy have a little more fun?" he suggested. "What do you think, Master?"

"Yeah," the Master agreed, "he's a growing boy, he needs all the protein he can get."

"And besides," added Clay, "he's got a big test this evening, so he can use all the practice you can give him."

"Right," said the Milk Master, "let's let him work on a cheeselog."

excerpt from
THE MILK FARM
MEMBERS' HANDBOOK

The Layout of The Milking Barn

Here is a typical day's layout of the stalls and the mancows in The Milking Barn. On either side of the long center aisle there are 5 stalls, each about 12 feet square, except for a few half-size stalls. In each 12×12 stall three studcows are strapped to their stations, ready for milking.

From the front door down the left side:
STALL A: Pure Whole Milk. Station 1: "Sweetheart."
Station 2: "Rusty." Station 3: "Protein Bill."
STALL B: Light Creamers. Station 1: "Half 'n' Half."
Station 2: "Plain Sam." Station 3: "Coffee Dan."
STALL C: Heavy Creamers. Station 1: "Thick Jim."
Station 2: "Custard Boy." Station 3: "Chocolate Syrup."
STALL D-ONE: Daily Specials. "Gusher" and "Milkshaker."
STALL D-TWO: Private Closed Box.
STALL E: Skimmers: Station 1: "Juicy Joe." Station 2:
"Young Squirt." Station 3: "One-Percent."
STALL F: The Cheese Box: Station 1: "Butterball."
Station 2: "Cheddar Jack." Station 3: "Cheesecake Charlie."

At the Rear is The Refreshment Bar, the toilet, and
The 5-6-7 Room.
From the rear, coming back toward the front, on the right side of the aisle:
STALL G: Veteran Stock: Station 1: "Boss." Station 2:
"Ropey." Station 3: "Gentleman."
STALL H: Ball Milking: Station 1: "Red Apples."
Station 2: "Leather Bags." Station 3: "Dangler."
STALL I: The Punishment Stall: Stations to be announced.

STALL J: Traditional Milking: Station 1: "Mother Teat."
Station 2: "Udderboy." Station 3: "Bulltit."
STALL K: Exotics and Experimentals: Station 1:
"Tokyo Tak." Station 2: "Strawberry Nips." Station 3:
"The Sheik."
STALL L: New Stock: Station 1: "Jiffy." Station 2:
"Sweetmeat." Station 3: "Wildman."

Mancows on standby in the stock lounge: "Angeltit," "Smart
Alec," "Pasteurized Pete," "Buster," "Milkbucket," and
"Yank."

CHAPTER FOUR

Cheesecakes and Milkshakes

They led me to a stall near the rear of the center aisle. The sign at the front read:

STALL F

The Cheese Box

Station 1   Butterball

Station 2   Cheddar Jack

Station 3   Cheesecake Charlie

Inside there were three cows strapped to the walls of the stall. At first glance they weren't much to look at: the guy nicknamed Butterball was a bit pudgy and Cheddar Jack was a very thin, lanky type with yellow-blonde hair, parted in the center and falling along the sides of his narrow, mean-looking face almost to his bony shoulders. But all of them had long, uncut dicks with plenty of loose foreskin, which was stretched down and tied off, over the cockheads. There were no other customers in the box at the moment, so we walked around and looked at each of the cheese-makers.

"The Cheeseboys have accumulated 2 days' worth of ripe head-cheese inside these tied-off foreskins," the Milk Master explained, holding up the semi-hard tube of Cheddar Jack for me to look at. "Except for a straw inserted to let them piss twice a day, they haven't washed or pulled back their skins that whole time. Each day they've been handmilked in the Lab with their skins tied shut so the good creamcheese can pile up inside that balloon of flesh around their dickheads. By the time they get strapped into the Cheese Box they've each got a ripe tangy load of suckcheese for their pullers. Of course, they're only good for one pull, because once they've been sucked there's no cheese left, so there's a sur-charge for the cheeselogs, but we'll waive that for you, Teddy, since you're a new high school graduate!"

"We both appreciate that," Clay admitted, with a little laugh.

They led me over to Station 3 where Cheesecake Charlie stood

glaring at us. He was a short guy with platinum white hair in a very short brush cut. It must have been bleached because his pubic hair was brown. His skinny dick hung about seven inches down between his white thighs; another two inches of foreskin was tied shut over the head, but the skin was a little bloated, as if there was a full load of something coating the mushroom shape beneath.

"This will give you a chance to practice your tongue work some more, Teddy," encouraged the Master, "because it takes a lot of expert licking under that foreskin to get the cheese out."

I wasn't sure I liked the idea of eating two-day-old cumcheese, but Clay firmly pressed me down to my knees from the rear, while the Master held up Cheesecake Charlie's puckered rosette of foreskin to my mouth. Before I could say anything the Milk Master squeezed my cheeks with his other hand and popped that puckered nipple into my lips.

"Just tongue it a little, at first," he ordered, "get the sensation of that cheesetube in your mouth. Do you feel how that cockhead sort of squishes around in the creamcheese that's tied up in there?"

I nodded my head and explored the strange texture and weight of the cheeseteat that now began to leak just the tiniest hint of something sour onto my tongue. I wanted to pull back, but Clay held my head down on the meat, and the Master rubbed the foreskin nipple around my mouth cavity, over my teeth and into the space between my cheeks and my gums. More of the sourness leaked out, and my mouth began to water so that drool ran down my chin onto my chest.

"It's cheese, Teddy," soothed the Milk Master, "you like cheese, don't you? Just give it a try. Bite down lightly on the string that's tying the skin shut and pull it, working it down off the nipple."

I felt the string begin to move forward, squeezing the gathered foreskin tighter, until it popped off, leaving the dick untied, ready to give up all that stored-up cheese inside. The Master put his fingers at my lips and pulled the string away, then he pushed the head of the cheeseteat a little deeper onto the middle part of my tongue. Now every movement of my mouth brought new tastes: first there was a sweet sourness, like a bite of creamy lemon cheesecake; then a touch of something tangy, like goat cheese, but all soft and runny. Gradually as I began to be braver about sticking my tongue up into those foreskin lips I sensed more solid pieces

of stuff emerging and dissolving in my drool. As each little chunk of the harder headcheese began to crumble in my mouth, fresh explosions of ripeness hit my tastebuds.

"Now get your tongue right down inside that tube, Teddy," directed the Milk Master. "Move it around between the dickhead and the outer hood. That's where the really good stuff is. . . . Keep going. . . . Push your pricklicker over the ridge of the crown and swab it all around to dig out your treat."

Clay's strong hands still held my shoulders and I could feel his warm breath on my chin as he watched me pull Cheesecake Charlie. "Let me hear you say 'yummmm,' " he whispered into my ear. "Let me hear you pigout on that cheeselog."

I began to make slurping sounds. There was something addictive to the sharp taste that came from the head of Cheesecake Charlie's meat. The more cheese I dug out with my tongue, the more I wanted. And the more I got, the more my saliva streamed, until my chin and my chest were covered with a sticky mixture of spermcheese and spit. Finally I couldn't control myself. I grabbed the shaft and skinned the flesh back off the head so that I would gobble noisily at it with an appetite that just kept getting stronger as I swallowed every stinging nugget.

At last I realized that there didn't seem to be any cheese left on that hot teat. At the same time I heard Cheesecake Charlie huffing and puffing, and felt him straining forward against the straps that bound him to the wall, until he shot a load of fresh, noncheesy milk, like a spicy mouthwash after the heady cheese feast. I kept on suckling that long, loose nipple of flesh, pulling it out gently with my teeth, taking it between my forefingers and thumbs and opening it into a tube to cover my tongue, stabbing down at the cheesehold on the shrinking cockhead.

Again, the Milk Master had to pull me away from my fun. "You're just like all young milkers," he laughed, "you never want to stop."

"I want to pull Cheddar Jack," I pleaded. "Let me do him too, please."

Clay lifted me to my feet. "No, Teddy, we've got a better treat for you." He looked at the Master, who was unstrapping Cheesecake Charlie so that a Milking Assistant could lead him back to the staff compound since he was through for the day. "I think he

deserves a milkshake, don't you, Milk Master?"

"That's fine with me, if you think he's up to it." The Master took hold of my wrists and turned my hands over so he could examine my palms. "Do you think he's aggressive enough yet to whip the Milkshaker up?"

Clay snorted, "Master, this little jerkpuppy beats his meat four or five times a day. All he needs is a little education and a little discipline to make him a champion masturbator."

I blushed a hot red at hearing Clay reveal the pitiful secrets of my so-called sex life to an expert like the Milk Master. Besides I doubted that I needed any "education" in jerking off. So far as I was concerned I was already a pro at it. God knows I'd had enough practice!

*　*　*

As we came out of the Cheese Box we noticed that a small crowd had gathered in the stall opposite with the sign saying "Veteran Stock." The Master explained that a "veteran" cow was one nearing the end of his three-year service in the stalls. "Veterans have been juiced so many times they need some really rough work to produce a milky load. It's still in there—you've just got to chow down on them long and hard to get it out." As we joined the group, we saw that one of the customers was giving a sort of demonstration as he worked on a cow named "Boss."

"This customer is a great milker," explained the Master, "and his specialty is 'Gag-Ring Milking.' This is way out of your league, Teddy, but take a listen anyway; find out what the future may hold for you."

The client was kneeling in front of a mature, lanky cow with a ropey, muscular look. He was holding the cow's teat in his hand as he talked. "You can see that this older studbull has a nice seven inch cock with a fat stalk, but one of those pointed, tapering heads. It fits right down my gullet just to my gag muscle. Now, I've been practicing my squeeze techniques with my gag-ring just on the head of this dick for the last fifteen minutes. I keep the head down my throat and give it a series of quick, sharp squeezes."

He swallowed the cow's teat smoothly and we would see his throat contracting and releasing around the head. Then he came off the teat suddenly. "This cow wants to cum like crazy. You see

how he's sweating, and breathing hard? I must already have squeezed a half a cup of precum out of him. But when I feel his teat lips start to swell and flutter, I take his big bags in my two hands and twist them hard, till he bellows—like that! Oh, yeah, I love to hear this bull yell: that sends his milk right back up into his nut reservoirs, where it builds up as more and more cream starts pressing to come out. After another thirty minutes or so of gag muscle practice I'll let him shoot. He'll be shaking all over, desperate to squirt, and when it comes it will be a feast, I'm telling you. But this is the important thing—the best part is that I'll have learned a lot of new tricks in that hour before I let him blow. Come on in a little closer and let me show you something."

We all moved farther into the box, some of the guys in front going down on their knees to see better. The milker took a good grip on the shaft of the cow's teat and squeezed it so that the head began to swell a little. "I've learned that there are three positions on the head of this cock where I can work the squeeze muscle in my throat. One is right behind this coronal ridge here." He took the cow's cockhead in his thumb and forefinger and twisted them around the ledge where the glans met the shaft. "My throat muscle sort of grabs the shaft just behind that ridge and locks down on it: then I do a set of hard contractions right at that point, pumping it hard with my gag-ring so that his cockhead swells until it's almost twice its normal size. You've got to breathe very carefully during this technique or you'll pass out."

He swallowed the dick once again and we knew from the cow's straining that his shaft was getting a good squeezing. When the milker came off the meat, we saw that the head was greatly expanded and flushed a bright purple-red. "Now the second position on his cockhead," continued the milker, "is just about halfway down on the meatus, right at the center point between the coronal ridge and the cocklips. Here the flesh is soft and you can do a slow squeeze-and-release routine, practically compressing that dickhead until it's shaped like a little hour-glass—a big rounded tip, a tiny nipped-in waist, and a swelling bulge down to the ridge. This is good for letting the cow know that you're getting ready to work the cocklips. It captures lots of blood up in those sensitive lips and the whole tip starts to inflate and get a little numb. Because the third and best area for the gag muscle to squeeze is the tip itself."

He pinched the very end of the cow's teat between two finger tips, rotating the compressed cocklips in tiny circles until the guy began to whimper. "See, that's what you've got to try to do with your gag muscle—squeeze your throat ring down to a tight circle, less than a half an inch across, so that the cow's cumhole lips are caught in it and bulge out through it. Then you flutter—make quick little contractions right on those puffy lips. That is fantastic milking! I've had cows bawling at the top of their lungs for five minutes at a stretch while their milk spurts out squirt by squirt between each of the contractions. And after the shoot, when you've pulled your mouth off, you hold that teat up in your hand and take a good closeup view of the cockhead you've been draining. It will look like a great big round red cherry, but a cherry drooling just a rivulet of milky sap."

The milker laughed then at his own extravagant language. "Hell, I've got so carried away talking about it, that I've let this little milkteat start to go soft on me." He slapped the flank of the cow named "Boss" and began to handpump the guy's dick back to fullness. A gesture of his other hand shooed us away. "You guys go on and do your own milking now, I've got work to do here." We all began to move off as he sank the veteran stud's teat back down his throat and began to ripple his gag muscle once again on the turgid head. "Boss" groaned and let his body sag back against the wall: he clearly knew that he was in for a long, hard session.

* * *

I was beginning to feel thirsty for another swig of manmilk. Listening to the "Gag-Ring" specialist had been a little too much like sitting through one of Miss Thurston's Oral Hygiene lectures in school. I wanted some action! We walked back to the half-sized stall where we had watched the customer pull the Gusher earlier. Now the sign in front said *The Milkshaker*, and a different guy was on view. This time the boycow was seated on a high sort of barstool, with his torso strapped tightly against the metal stanchion behind, running from floor to roof. His wrists and his ankles were cuffed and pulled back with chains toward the rear wall so that his trim body seemed to arch forward presenting his dick and his balls for easy access at the end of the stool. The milkteat and the creambags on Milkshaker were a wonder. The kid was

young, slim, and sensitive looking, with a long thin nose and sensuously curved lips. His eyes were dark and pleading and his tousled black hair hung down into his eyebrows, giving him an exhausted look, as if he had been worked hard before being tied to the milking stool. But that slender, boyish body was contradicted by the massive long meat and the luscious hanging balls arching from his crotch.

We stopped about six feet in front of him and looked at the exciting image he offered: a fragile handsome boy attached to a gigantic penis and monster testicles.

"This is The Milkshaker," announced the Master. He's very special. He can only produce twice a day, with at least a two hour rest between each pull, so there's a surcharge for milking him, but he's worth it. You see he's got a fat, nine-inch teat and full, plump bags. This cow's not for sucking: this one gets his teat beaten and slapped and jerked, and his balls squeezed and tugged until he makes a big vanilla milkshake for you."

"Teddy, I think I'll leave you in the Master's care for this one," Clay interrupted. "I saw a juicy little teat over in the New Stock stall that I'd like to drain."

"Go ahead, Mr.B.," encouraged the Master. "You're probably talking about that new kid with the pink dick that looks like it's never been touched. He's just come from the six-week conditioning program, but I've got to warn you that he's a quick-shooter. His juice is sweet, but it squirts pretty fast. That's why we call him Jiffy. The good thing is that we let you pull him twice in a row without resting, and his second shot is bigger and sweeter than his first."

"That sounds like just what I'm looking for," said Clay, as he moved off to the other side of the aisle.

The Milk Master moved me toward The Milkshaker. The stool was high enough that I could work on him standing up, giving me a chance to watch his face when I wanted to.

The Master looked at me with a knowing smile. "I suppose you think you're a first-class dickjerker, Teddy?"

"I don't want to brag," I smirked, "but I have had a lot of experience at it." The Master reached down and took my prick in his hand. He looked it over closely. "Yes, I can see that this meat has had a lot of work, but I think I can teach you a few tricks."

"If you say so, Sir," I said, obediently, always ready to learn new ways to pop my load.

"Okay, Teddy, grab the Shaker's teat with your right hand down near the root. Keep the edge of your hand jammed into his groin so that as much of his prick as possible sticks out for you to work on. You can squeeze it tighter than that. Grip it so the five inches that still stick out from your fist swell up and get puffy. That's it."

It felt good to have a dick other than my own in my hand at last. I squeezed as hard as I could on it and watched the big veins on the shaft swell up, and the massive head turn beet red.

The Milk Master continued the lesson in handmilking. "Now put the palm of your left hand up and just let that dick lie across it."

I felt the hot shaft and the moist crown rest heavily in my hand.

"Now beat it against the palm of your hand, hard," the Master ordered. . . . "No, no, Teddy, I said *beat* it. Whip that thing down with a smack against your left hand. . . . Do it again. . . . And again! Go on, keep slapping it hard—don't worry about his whimpering, that's just his motor getting warmed up."

I slammed the kid's long red meat repeatedly against my palm, watching him close his thick-lashed eyes and grit his teeth, as he made little whining sounds in his throat.

"Pay attention to your milking," the Master barked. "Now jerk down with your fist until you make a little false foreskin around the head of his meat. And skin it back. Jerk it again. Do that about a dozen times, Teddy. Work that meat."

I tugged at that big dick as if I wanted to pull it out by the root. I liked the way his shaftskin came down in a roll halfway over the big head when I pulled on it. The guy now began to groan and writhe against his straps.

"Beat him some more. Slap your palm with that milkteat. Try counting the slaps so you get into a rhythm. Give him ten cock-slaps against your hand, then jerk him hard ten times, then go back to the slaps, then the jerks, and keep that up for a while." The Master kept me at my work as I got more and more excited about really manhandling the kid's massive meat.

"Look at those big balls start to churn, Teddy. That milk's start-ing to froth up in those big babies. This cow is going to feed you

good, if you just keep working him hard." The Master seemed to be getting excited as well. I saw him pawing at the bulge crawling down the leg of his trousers. "Now, we'll step up the pace," he panted. "Circle the base of his dick with just your thumb and forefinger. . . . Tighten down hard, Teddy. . . . Now whip that cock around like a helicopter blade. . . . Keep it circling. . . . Harder, Teddy, harder! Circle it in the other direction. . . . Whip that thing, baby, whip that teat."

The boy started to breathe so heavily that his chest heaved against the black leather straps holding him to the pole. "Oh, yeah," shouted the Master, "he's starting to wind up good. Look, Teddy, even the precum is frothy!" Honey-colored strings of prick-lube began to fly out of the hole in the dickhead which I kept whipping until my wrist began to ache. The Shaker began to pull wildly at the wrist and ankle chains which kept his body arched backward, tight as a bow.

The Milk Master crowded in even closer to us, egging me on, telling me how to force the guy's cream out. "Come on, Teddy, we're getting there. Put both your fists on his teat and really pump it hard. . . . Keep pumping! Pull it up as far and as fast as you can. He's starting to get to the edge. Hear that groan, like some stud that wants milking real bad? That's your sign." He had his own dick out now, mauling it in both his hands. "Keep pumping! Get your face down over the head. Open your mouth wide and get your tongue out, because you're just about to get the best milk-shake you ever had!"

With a low guttural sound, that soon became a high-pitched howl, the Milkshaker blew! His cumspray frothed out and bubbled up into my greedy mouth. His milk was fizzy and sweet, like hot cream soda. It kept spraying out, misting my lips and chin with warm sperm. At the same time I felt on my right cheek other splatters of hot milk. The Milk Master was cumming on my face too!

But even now, at the moment of his own climax, the Milk Master kept up his instructions. "Lick the head, Teddy," he gasped, rubbing his own hot cockhead in the sperm he had shot on my cheek, "but keep your mouth open while you tongue it. Let the froth spew up into your throat, fill your cheeks with it."

Believing that the Milkshaker had shot his load, I started to pull away. "No, no," cried the Master, "don't back off, he's not

finished. This cow will bubble on for a long time. Just keep jerking that shaft with both hands whenever the flow seems to be dying down. Yeah, there it comes again, another big mouthful. Keep on, Teddy, get it all."

I drank several more sweet dollops of vanilla-flavored spume, but even then the Master wouldn't let me free the Milkshaker from my grasp. "Now, when you think this milkboy might be all squeezed out, Teddy, take that spongy dick in your fist again and give it one more good whack across your palm—pow!—that's it! Then squeeze it hard, starting at the base and pressing up with your fingers toward the tip and—there! One more spoonful of foam!"

I siphoned off this last offering. By now the flavor of the guy's cum was more subtle, like a thin custard. The Milk Master was relentless. "Let's see if he's holding back. Smack it and squeeze it again, Teddy. Oh, yeah! This cumpuppy is holding out on you. Look at that! Another good tongueful of prime juice."

I got into the spirit of the action, and attacked the Shaker's milkhole savagely, pretending I was angry that he was keeping back any of his cream from my hungry mouth. The Milk Master had one last instruction. "Now, just to show this baby that everything he's got is yours to drink, take those fat balls in your fist, Teddy. Grip them up at the top, near the base of his meat and slide your hand down so those two big milknuts get tight in their sack. . . . Good boy! Take your other hand, now, and squeeze those balls— not too hard—just enough to make him moan. . . . That's it! Okay, Teddy, here's the procedure. You've got to squeeze and release those udders in a steady rhythm about fifty times."

I started my count, liking the feel of soft ripe manfruit beneath the velvety skin of their sack. The Master pushed my head down toward the still swollen head of the teat which he held up toward me. "Get your mouth on his milkhead again. Make a tight seal with your lips right on that little milkhole, and suction like crazy, Teddy. Pretty soon he's going to squirt a little fizzy droplet right on your tongue. . . . Do you taste that? Keep your squeeze-and-release trick going, and after a while he's going to give you one creamy drop for almost every squeeze. Sometimes he'll be good for another hundred drops, and, man, that last juice is the best."

Well, the Milkshaker wasn't good for a hundred more drops of

cream, but he kept squirting long enough to give me my fill of his delicious cum. When I finally stopped squeezing his balls in that hypnotic rhythm and stood back to look at the remains of my work, he stared back at me through heavy-lidded eyes with an ironic little smirk on his lips, as if to say "Had enough, cocksucker?" His nine inches arched down between his legs, slick and puffy, with just a thread of clear aftercum dangling from the dewy milklips on the head. When the Milking Assistant came forward to take him down from his chains, the Shaker staggered as he stood up, and sagged into the man's arms. The burly Assistant slung him, belly down, over his shoulder and took him through the door at the back of the stall.

"Nice work, Teddy," the Master said, approvingly. "We like a milker who lets the cows know who's in control. Come on, let's find Mr. B and see if he got fed as well as you did."

*　　*　　*

We found Clay relaxing on a deep leather sofa, looking into a stall where there was a lot of activity. He was idly massaging his big dick and he had a satisfied smile on his face. He waved us down beside him, me in the middle again, and the Milk Master on my other side.

"What's that on your cheek, Teddy?" asked Clay, taking my chin in his hand and turning my face toward him. "It looks like you tried to take the Milkshaker's load in the wrong hole."

The Milk Master laughed. "I'm afraid I'm responsible for that little mess. This dickpounder got me so hot when he was whipping up the Shaker's froth, that I just couldn't keep from creaming him myself. Shall I wipe it off?"

"No, no," Clay said, "his mug looks good smeared with a big load of cum like that." He put his hand up and smoothed the sticky stuff all around my face, finally rubbing some into my lips like a creamy chapstick. It felt good, because, in fact, my lips were starting to get a bit chapped from all the sucking I'd been doing that afternoon.

"I see you like to watch the traditional guys, Mr. B.," commented the Milk Master. He directed my attention toward the stall in front of us. The sign read:

STALL J
Traditional Milking
Station 1   Babe
Station 2   Bulltit Blue
Station 3   Udder-Boy

In this stall the cows were on their hands and knees so the milkers could pull their big hanging teats from the side, like a calf at his mother's udder, or from the rear. One guy had drawn Bulltit Blue's long, loose milkmeat back hard through the stud's legs, letting his big balls drape down on either side of the reversed dick. The milker's mouth and face were working over the whole area from asshole, to balls, to dickhead: as he sucked that swollen head, his nose nudged up into the bull's ass-crack, stimulating him to press back into the face that was milking him.

Another customer was lying on his back, with his head looking up at the big milkteat hanging down from Udder-Boy's crotch. The long, slender nipple dangled at the milker's mouth, and he nursed it like a baby with a bottle. The cows were chained by the neck to large rings on the walls of the stall, and their wrist-cuffs were tied down to smaller rings in the floor so their movement was restricted. The massive bodybuilder named Babe, who was being sucked savagely by a milker coming at him from the side, also had a rod strapped between his knees which kept his thighs opened very wide so his sucker had free access to his bullnuts.

After a while the Milk Master and Clay started to get really hot and hard. They had been working my prick and my nuts pretty roughly while they watched and commented on the milkers' techniques. Now they made me stand up, while they moved to sit side by side on the couch. Then they had me lie back down across their thighs, face up. My head and my legs hung down on the sofa seat on either side of them, but my crotch and my chest were raised across their laps, and I could feel their hard dicks throbbing against my back and nosing up into the cleavage between my ass-cheeks. The Milk Master leaned his face down and grazed on my flopping penis, like a bull at its feed while he watched the action in the stall, and Clay chowed down on my tits, nipping at them with his teeth and stabbing them with his tongue until they started to sting and swell.

Every time I began to breathe heavily and stiffen up my body

because I was going to shoot my load, they stopped and punished my dick and tits with slaps and bites to bring me back down.

Then one of the Milking Assistants walked down the aisle swinging a big cowbell, calling out, "Five minutes, Gentlemen, the afternoon milking session will be over in five minutes. The evening session will commence at 9:00 p.m. Five minutes to closing, Gentlemen." There were groans and curses from milkers who knew they couldn't finish off the cows they were milking by closing time, but gradually everybody began to move slowly toward the big doors at the front of the barn. As we walked I saw other intriguing stall signs and cow nicknames. Everywhere the Milking Assistants were unstrapping the milkstuds from their stations and leading them off toward the back of the room.

As we came to the front I looked into Rusty's stall, where I had started this new life just about four hours ago. He was still strapped in, so apparently he hadn't been pulled the maximum four times during the session. His meaty dick looked swollen and red and his milkbags had a purplish tint to them. The Milk Master saw me looking at Rusty.

"You liked that little cow, didn't you, Teddy?" he asked. "That's always the way. Your first pull is a special one. There's still a couple of minutes till closing; go over and give that teat one last lick. We'll wait."

I went into the stall. Rusty looked at me and smiled. He didn't say anything because he wasn't allowed to talk to his milkers. I took his puffy red teat in my hand and knelt down to look at it closely. This was the first cock I had sucked, just a little while ago, but already I felt like an experienced milker. I examined Rusty's equipment with a new expertise. It was smooth, without many veins or marks on it. The head was satiny and the ridge was deep, almost a quarter-inch. I knew now that this gave the milker something to grip onto with his lips so he could pull the whole shaft forward and wash over the dickhead with his tongue at the same time. A thick, deep ridge around the crown was a quality highly prized in a milkdick. I was happy to know that my own dick had a big ledge around the head, but I was beginning to wonder if I'd ever feel a man's lips on it! I noticed that Rusty's milkballs were only medium-sized compared to some of the other juicebags I had seen that day. But even in their well-used purplish state, after a

full session at his station, they had a fresh look. I wanted to ask Rusty how long he'd been a mancow. I thought maybe he was just new to the Farm. I didn't know, then, anything about the rigorous training that all the cows had to go through before serving in The Milking Barn.

But I realized I was wasting time just looking, so I opened my mouth and let my tongue lap lazily over Rusty's shiny dickhead. He hummed in his throat as if he really liked that. He leaked a drop of spicy lube and I responded eagerly by burying my nose right into his ginger crotchhair, with his teat firmly in my throat.

The Milk Master touched me on the shoulder and warned, "That's it, Teddy, time to go."

I stood up, looked Rusty in the eye, and gave his dick a friendly farewell squeeze. He smiled and winked at me.

As we went into the front lobby to put our terrycloth robes back on, I asked the Master if I could pull Rusty again that evening. Clay said that he had other plans for me that evening, so I asked if I could pull Rusty on the next day, Saturday. That's when I found out that each cow got a day's rest after a day spent in the stalls. Rusty would recuperate and the Laboratory staff would build up his milk supply in the staff compound, a special separate area for all the employees.

"But, if you're a real good boy," promised the Milk Master, "maybe someday soon you'll get to see the staff stables for yourself."

"That would be great!" I said.

The Milk Master and Clay both laughed a lot when I said that!

excerpt from
THE MILK FARM
MEMBERS' HANDBOOK

Hotel Room Service List

The following services are available on a 24 hour basis.

Room Boy. Cleanup boy for quick relief when you come back horny from a long Milking Barn session. Room Boys are available for suck service only: they cannot be fucked; their meat can be manhandled to the cum-point but they are not allowed to climax. Any client who forces a Room Boy to cum may be denied future Room Boy service. The prohibition against climaxing is necessary to keep our Room Boys at maximum horniness and to give their sucking abilities that extra Milk Farm "edge." Maximum 30 minute stay.

Cocktail and Nut Service. The Waiter will mix the special Cocktails of the Day in your room and also deliver Cocktail Nuts for maximum 30 minute use. Some Milk Farm cocktail specialties: Extra-dry Pissvermouth Martini; Champagne Cocktail made with a sugar cube soaked in tangy precum; the Milk Farm Margarita sipped between licks on the salt en-crusted cockhead of an accompanying cocktail boy; and the most exotic of all, the Milk Farm Man-Pousse Café—layers of fresh mancream alternated with layers of liqueur-flavored precum—expensive but worth every penny! Our Nut Boys are chosen for the plump firmness of their equipment and they are trained to take some rough fist-cracking and teeth-crunching. They may be handcuffed, or they may be ordered to gather their nuts in their own fists and present them for you to munch on.

Sushi Snack. Fresh, raw oriental shrimpboys. Each order consists of three morsels with their own special sauce and

saki-piss if desired. The Room Waiter will hold up the fresh sea-tangy sexmeat with chopsticks for you to nibble at. At least one of the sushi dicks will be wrapped in rice and seaweed paper for you to bite off, stimulating the quivering fishstick beneath to spurt its tart cumsauce. For an after-course, the boys' nut-oysters can be dipped into a hot horseradish sauce and sucked clean to the accompaniment of cool sips of Japanese beer.

Barber. Try a stimulating full body-shave (excluding head and eyebrows) from our skilled Barber.

Face and Mouth Massage. Refreshing after a strenuous day in the milking stalls. Our masseur will bring to your room a padded massage table and a specially trained massage milkcow. You'll lie back on the comfortable table and the masseur will bring the milkcow to your side: the cow's arms will be tied behind him and his large spongy teat will be firmly grasped by the masseur and brought to your face. These massage cows have been conditioned to remain semi-soft during the manipulation and they leak a constant stream of golden precum. The masseur rubs the big malleable man-teat over your face, letting the natural lubricant smooth the way. After this preliminary treatment, the masseur jerks the teat firmly until it shoots a creamy, non-salty milk which he then massages into your skin, still using the big teat as a tool. He grasps the plump velvety head of the mancow's meat and uses it to smooth lines at the eyes and on the forehead. Special attention is given to the mouth area and the lips; the masseur gently pulls back your lips and massages your gums with the leaking meatus. The fleshy tube is rolled on your neck and jawline and the cream is rubbed up into your hairline, creating a milk-mask which tightens your skin as it dries. Two cucumber slices soaked in cock cream are placed over your eyes and a warm moist towel is wrapped around your face and

head. As you drift off for a short nap a lipboy is brought in to service your own cock and balls gently. Before he leaves the lipboy unwraps the towel from your head and licks off all the cum residue from your face with his versatile tongue. Room Service will also deliver to your suite the Milk Farm Health Shake—vanilla yogurt, crushed pineapple and half a cup of fresh frozen cum frothed in a blender and served in a tall glass. Foot massage, nipple massage, and rump massage with special attention to the pucker hole are also available.

Golden Shower Service. Lavish warm shower of light high-quality piss, including a cum scalpmassage and shampoo, if desired.

CHAPTER FIVE

Room Service

Clay and I went up to our room to rest before dinner. He asked me if I was having a good time on my birthday. I told him it was the best time of my life, but that there was only one problem.

"What's that, Teddy?"

"I'm awfully horny, Clay," I complained. "Look at my dick. It just stays swollen and leaks gunk all the time. I really need to jerk off, so I won't be so embarrassed in front of everybody."

"Teddy," he promised, "if you just keep holding off, you'll have the thrill of your life when I do let you pop your nuts. Besides, nobody cares about your hard, dripping dick—in fact, they all like it—a lot!"

I wasn't exactly satisfied with that, but I realized there wasn't much point in arguing, so I went in to take a shower. Clay came right in with me, just to make sure I didn't get off while I was under the spray. He soaped me all over, even probing his slick finger up into my asshole. My whole body stiffened up when he did that, and he stopped right away, saying that I shouldn't worry about assplay, that I wasn't "ready" for that yet. Then he had me soap him all over. That was the first time I had ever touched his cock and balls. I got excited and knelt down, thinking that maybe I would milk him right there in the shower using my new suck skills. But he pulled me back up.

"Not yet, suckboy," he said, holding me off, "that comes later. You'll get all the daddy dick you can take later tonight."

I was sleepy after all the pleasure and stimulation of the afternoon, so I laid down on the bed to nap. Clay turned on the TV and sat down in one of the big easy chairs to watch it, throwing his leg over one arm of the chair and casually playing with his meat. As I dozed off, I realized it wasn't a regular TV channel he was watching—at least, not unless the Soaps have started letting the "hunks" push their cocks in each others' faces!

About half an hour later I woke when someone knocked at the

door. Clay opened it to let in a Room Waiter dressed in nothing but a short black waiter's jacket and a black jockstrap. He had a rolling tray with some glasses and bottles on it.

"You ordered the Special Cocktail Service, Sir?"

"Yes," Clay answered, "my boy and I would like to try your Cocktail of the Day. What's today's drink?"

"Our Special Room Service Cocktail this evening is a Classic Dry Martini with a Milk Farm variation. It's very dry Tanqueray Gin with just a hint of piss-vermouth and a cumsoaked lemon twist."

Clay looked at me. "What do you think, Teddy? Can you handle a grown-up drink like that?"

I'd had beer and cheap wine, and sometimes the kids would drink rum and coke at parties, but a martini was way beyond my experience. "I'd like to try one," I announced, bravely.

"That's the spirit, boy," said Clay. "Waiter, do your stuff."

The waiter opened the green bottle of gin and poured quite a bit, more than enough for two drinks each, into a shaker of ice. Then he pulled aside the pouch of his jockstrap, and produced a long, rosy pink prick. He held the shaker under it.

"Say 'when,'" he said with a grin, and squirted a splash of clear piss from his dick into the gin and ice.

Clay laughed and called, "When!" and the waiter put his tube back into his jock, then stirred the piss and gin gently. He poured the mixture into two frosted martini glasses he took from a little ice chest on his cart. Then he picked up a twist of yellow lemon rind from a small dish and dipped it into a flat saucer of something white and creamy.

"This cum is fresh today," he assured us. "The Bar Boys are milked every morning and their juice is refrigerated." He dropped cumsoaked lemon twists into the glasses and gave us each one, waiting for us to taste. Clay sipped his, sloshed it around on his tongue for a few seconds, and breathed, "Perfect!"

They both looked at me. "How about you, Teddy? What's your verdict?" Clay asked.

I took a tiny sip, I didn't know what to say because it wasn't like anything I had ever tasted before, but I liked the zing, so I said, "Perfect," just like Clay.

Smiling, the waiter pulled his prick out again and came toward me. "Are you sure you wouldn't like a little more vermouth, Sir?"

he teased.

"No, no," I stammered, to their mutual delight. "This is just fine."

"I've brought a Nutboy with me," the waiter offered, "if you want Cocktail Nut Service. He's just outside in the hall."

"Sure," accepted Clay, "send him in. It's this guy's first martini. He'd like some nuts to go with it."

The waiter went to the door and brought in a short, stocky kid wearing only a long T-shirt that said NUTBOY on it. "He's yours for thirty minutes, Gentlemen," the waiter explained. "Enjoy! I'll leave the pitcher with the rest of the martinis here on the bedside table."

As the waiter left, the Nutboy took off his shirt and stood at the foot of the bed. Clay and I were now sitting side by side on it with our backs up against the headboard, facing him. He had a street punk's short, muscular body, boyish, but tough. His touseled hair hung in bangs onto his forehead, into his eyes, giving him a shaggy unkempt look. He had the face of an urchin: small, mean eyes with the hint of a shiner beneath one of them, a short broad nose that looked as if it had been broken once or twice and small lips on a narrow pouting mouth.

We could see why he was called Nutboy. His cock was thick with a broad snubnosed head, uncut, the thick foreskin hugging the crown loosely, but his balls hung down about six or seven inches and they were round and plump like big plums or apricots. Both the dick and the nuts looked as if they had been given some rough treatment, maybe been tied up for hours at a time. Perhaps that's what gave him the wary, sullen look, as if he knew he was going to get mauled but was resigned to it.

"Where do you want me," he asked bluntly, "beside the bed or on it?"

Clay seemed a little angry about the kid's surly attitude. "We want you on the bed, between us, ballface."

He crawled up into the space between our bodies. "No, turn the other way," said Clay roughly, "put your head toward the foot of the bed and lie on your back. . . . Now spread your thighs wide." He picked up one of the Nutboy's sturdy calves and draped it across his own thighs. I did the same with the other leg, so that the Nutboy's eggs were lying loose in their leathery sack on the

bed just within a hand's reach of both of us.

I still wasn't sure what we were supposed to do, but Clay prompted me. He picked up his piss-martini and held it out towards me. I did the same with mine. "Here's to life after high school, baby. Cheers." I said thanks and we both took a sip. Then he reached down with his free hand and dug under the kid's nuts, giving them a hard squeeze. The kid jumped, but stayed where he was.

"These nuts are for our pleasure, Teddy. We can crack 'em, crunch 'em, chew 'em—do anything we want to 'em so long as we don't cause any permanent damage. Go ahead, give 'em a grope."

I took those big jewels in my hand and tugged down. Then I squeezed them really hard, three times in a row. It felt good.

We both took another big swallow of martini and then we really went to town on the kid's balls, mashing them like crazy. I'd twist the long sack in my fist while Clay would roll the firm nuggets in his fingers, pressing hard with his thumb. Then he'd use his hand to pull them down in their sack and I would take them in my palm and press them up hard against the edge of his big fist. The Nut-boy started to squirm and cry out. He even moved his hand down to his crotch as if to push his tormentors away. This got Clay really mad. He jumped out of bed and jerked the kid's wrists into the cuffs that were chained at the corners of the foot of the bed, so he couldn't resist us that way.

We finished our drinks and Clay poured us each another one from the pitcher. I was starting to feel light-headed and a little wild. I felt like I wanted to crack the Nutboy's balls wide open. I started to giggle when he gasped every time I compressed one of those spheres, like one of those rubber balls you use to build up your hand strength.

Clay said it was time to do some munching. He put his glass down on the bedside table after taking a big swig from it and leaned down to take one of the boyballs in his teeth. He began to nibble on it lightly. I put my drink down too and leaned forward to take the other ball in my mouth. We crunched and sucked and chewed on those succulent nutmeats until the Nutboy began to give little yelps and stiffen his whole body, straining against the cuff chains and trying to close his legs against our arms which held them wide open.

But all this time his dick got harder and harder, its fat head pushing out of the roll of foreskin, until it shot a geyser of jism up about a foot into the air. The warm eruption fell back down and splattered my face where I was nuzzling his sack. Clay sat up and gave the kid's dick a hard slap.

"Look what you've done to my boy, you ballbag! You've got his face all dirty with your scum."

He grabbed the guy's nutsack at the top and pulled down, making a round sponge of the two quivering ovals. He vigorously rubbed the cum off my cheek with that plush ball-sponge, then asked me if I wanted to lick it off the kid's nuts, still held down tight in his fist. I said I didn't want to lick it off, I wanted to *chew* it off! Clay liked that, so we both ate the Nutboy's cream off his own testicles with our hungry mouths.

After thirty minutes of nutplay, we reluctantly uncuffed the boy and let him get up. He stood again at the foot of the bed, his thighs widespread to let his steaming balls swing free. "I hope you enjoyed your cocktail nuts, Sirs," he whined. His rocks were red and so was his face. We thanked him and told him he was a good little Nutboy, and he walked out with a bowlegged limp that made us grin at each other. I had the feeling that cocktail boynuts were going to be one of my favorite snacks at The Milk Farm.

* * *

In the dining room that evening we sat at a round table with four other men. Ian and Carlo were in their early thirties and they were introduced as "lovers." This was the first time in my life I had ever heard two men openly name their relationship that way. Ian was an attorney, handsome in an intellectual way, with round glasses, and a long nose. He had perfectly shaped lips and deep green eyes. Carlo was a little younger, a landscape gardener, very tanned with long black hair, like a star in a TV western: his sexy good looks were a perfect complement to Ian's dryer, more sophisticated style.

Wesley was an older balding guy, a little chubby, with a round funny face and an outgoing friendly personality. He was a stock broker. These three men seemed to know Clay from previous visits to the Farm, and they all looked me over very closely when we sat down. Suddenly I did a double take: I knew who Wesley was! I'd watched him for almost half an hour on his knees in the 5-6-7

Room draining the gypsy stud's sperm. Wesley was the Master Milker with the infinite patience and the five-hundred repetition suck routines!

He saw me staring and said, "Have we met somewhere before, Sweetheart?" I felt my face grow hot and I looked pleadingly at Clay. "Now you wouldn't by any chance be one of those voyeurs who crashed my 5-6-7 party this afternoon, would you?" With a wry grin he addressed the table at large. "I blow a quarterly dividend check from my stock holding in The Pleasure Corporation on one special suck session, and have to share it with some horny snoopers! I should get a discount for providing entertainment."

"Watching you drain some poor cow dry isn't my idea of entertainment," Ian riposted. "Besides, we all know that you're the richest guy in the room, so button your beautiful cum-stained lips!"

In the midst of the laughter and joking that followed the fourth man was introduced simply as the Major. He was a very tough looking military type with a greying blonde crewcut and muscular arms. The other men were dressed in slacks and shirts, casually, although Ian had on a tie and Wesley had a light summer jacket as well, but the Major looked as if he had just come from the barracks in army camouflage pants and a khaki T-shirt that accentuated the bloat of his biceps. Clay had let me wear a denim shirt and a pair of pleated cotton pants, but no underwear, so my hard dick and swollen balls hung down one leg in a lump, and soon there was a wet spot where my cocklips kept weeping.

Conversation was mostly about the afternoon's experiences in The Milking Barn. Ian asked me if this was my first time for manmilking and Carlo described how he just about went insane on his first visit to the Barn, trying to suck every cow in the place in three hours.

"He burped up cum all night long," joked Ian.

"How would you know, buddy?" Carlo retorted. "If I remember correctly you had your tongue up my asshole most of that night."

They teased the Major for spending the whole afternoon in the Ball Milking Stall. I learned that this was the stall where mancows got their milkbags well sucked. The Major, it seemed, had a taste for rough, tooth-grinding ballwork. But he had very little sense of humor about it and just told everybody to "shut their faggot

cuntmouths."

I had noticed that there were several young men standing at various places around the room at a kind of parade rest, except for one hand which they used to prime their dicks, keeping them in constant erection. Seeing me look at these "decorations," Wesley asked if I liked the taste of manjelly. When I said yes, he crooked his finger at one of these nude boys nearby and called, "Sauceboy!"

The guy came over to the table still fondling his meat. Wesley gestured toward me, "My young friend needs some hot cumsauce on his food," he ordered.

"Yes, Sir," the guy replied as he came to my side. He thrust his crotch over my plate, pulled his dick hard about three times and shot a splash of thick white cum right onto my New York cut, medium-rare steak. After one spurt, he pinched his shaft hard right behind the curve of the head and said in a strained voice, "Would anyone else like some sauce?"

"Yes, give me a shot of that," said Wesley greedily.

The Sauceboy went to Wesley's plate and released his tight hold on his dick. Another spurt of cum shot out on Wesley's Lemon Sole.

The boy squeezed his dick shut again and gasped out, "Anyone else? I have a couple more servings if anyone is interested."

Carlo spoke up. "Hell, it would be a shame to waste it. Come over here and give it to me. But I'll just take it right from the source." He leaned down and put his lips to the boy's cumslit and sucked for about a minute while the guy finished shooting his load. When the Sauceboy had finished, he said, "Thank you, Sirs," to the table at large and started to walk away.

"Come back here, pussymouth," rasped the Major. "You've got that red strap around your neck for a reason. Your balls may be drained, but your throat's still good. Get down."

The boy knelt beside the Major's chair, lifted the tablecloth, and crawled out of sight. We heard the rustling of cloth, the sound of a zipper and then some wet, sucking noises. After a moment, nobody paid much attention. The conversation picked up again and Wesley started to rave about the magical Japanese milkboy he expected to pull in the Exotics Stall that evening.

I kept looking at the Major, who continued to eat his meal as if nothing was happening below.

Carlo was sitting next to me. "Gee, Teddy," he said, "I've dropped my napkin. Would you pick it up for me?" He was looking at me with a little smile on his face.

"Sure," I said. When I leaned down to get it, he pulled up the cloth so that I could see what was really going on. The Sauceboy had his face pushed deep into the Major's crotch, his nose smashed into a patch of wiry pubic hair. He wasn't moving his head in and out: he just held his mouth down on the Major's dick and seemed to be swallowing over and over on it.

"Thanks a lot, Teddy," Carlo grinned when I handed his napkin to him, happy to have given me a chance to satisfy my curiosity.

A little later the Major went rigid in his chair and his eyes glazed over for a minute. There were choking sounds from beneath the table.

"Uh-oh, it's chowtime in the Mess Hall," joked Wesley and everybody but the Major laughed.

Shortly after that the Sauceboy crawled out and shakily stood up. With a wet, flushed face he said, "Thank you, Sir," to the Major, before he walked off toward the kitchen.

I noticed that another Sauceboy had taken his place, ready to serve anyone who wanted that extra Milk Farm "touch." I saw one table make a Sauceboy shoot his stuff onto their hot rolls instead of butter. And after the main course, some of the Sauceboys became what Wesley called "Creamspouts" and stroked their rich liquids into coffee cups and brandy snifters.

When it was time for dessert at our table, Wesley begged Clay to let him buy me my first Milk Farm dessert.

"No," Clay said, "Teddy's going to get his dessert upstairs in our room. I've been saving up some special cumcustard for him. But thanks anyway, maybe tomorrow."

They all looked at me with renewed interest. When I stood up and revealed my trousers tented out obscenely with a spreading precum stain down my leg, the Major stared at it as if he wanted to eat me whole.

*   *   *

When we got to the room, Clay put the "Do Not Disturb" sign on the door and turned to me. "Sit down, Teddy," he commanded, "I want to ask you some questions."

I sat in one of the easy chairs next to the TV set, wondering if this was the "test" he had been talking about earlier. He sat in the other chair and just looked at me for a few moments. His eyes went to the massive mound of my crotch and the wet stain.

"Tonight I'm going to test you to see just how well you've learned your milking lessons," he began. "It's going to be a long examination and a difficult one, so I want to make sure you're ready for it. I want to make sure that you want it." He paused, then seemed to change the subject. "How do you feel after your first day at The Farm?"

"I feel fine," I answered, not knowing what he expected of me.

"You're not shocked at what you've been taught to do? You accept what goes on here as something you want to take part in?"

I thought for a minute before responding. "Some of the things seemed pretty radical at first, but I like The Farm. I'd like to come here often." I felt as if I'd made a crucial decision, just by saying that.

"Teddy, you're about to make a commitment by taking this test—a commitment to a lifestyle, not to just a few weekend sex trips. I want to give you a chance to walk away if it seems too strange to you. If you can't imagine sucking cock and having all kinds of sex with different guys for the rest of your life, now's the time to get out. I won't think any the worse of you, if you decide that this is not the way for you. You may think that having sex with guys is just something you're going through now, while you're young. You may not want to commit."

"Listen, Clay," I said, "ever since that night in my room with the porn magazine, you've known that I was attracted to men. And you know I've always let you feel me up when we were in the bathroom together and I would be drying off after my shower. I always went a lot further than that after you left. You must have realized that."

"Yes, Teddy," he admitted, "but that's not the same as getting down on your knees and eating semen out of a penis. Are you a cocksucker for sure?"

The blunt question shocked me a little. "I never thought of myself that way before, but I guess I am." I felt a wave of conviction rise in me. "Yeah, I'm a cocksucker for sure. I liked being on my knees in front of Rusty, and I liked digging Cheesecake Charlie's

spunk out of his foreskin, and I really liked whacking the Milk-shaker's big meat until it foamed. It felt good." I didn't know whether to go on or not. "The only thing is . . ." I stopped.

"What's 'the only thing,' Teddy?"

"I'd really like to get off, Clay. I don't have to get sucked, but it doesn't seem natural to have all this pressure building up inside me and not let it go. Can't I at least go into the bathroom and beat off?"

Clay was implacable. "If you pass the test, then we'll see about that. I promise you, Teddy, that you're going to shoot more cum than you've ever dreamed possible after tonight. It'll be part of your final graduation present tomorrow. But for now, we've got to fix you up so you don't squirt by accident during our session. Stand up and get all your clothes off."

He walked over to the bedside table and took something from the drawer while I peeled off my shirt and trousers. My dick had an inch of thick drool hanging off it. I stood there watching it lengthen in one long thread and attach itself to my leg. Clay came up in front of me and held up a leather strap about three inches wide. He sat on the edge of the bed. "Bring that horny suckmeat over here," he ordered sternly.

I walked over to him and stood between his widespread legs. My meat was just about at his chin level. He grasped my dick and my balls right at the root where my pubic hair curls up. He pulled the whole package forward and draped the strap over the big pipe of flesh created by the force of his hand stretching me. Then he snapped the ends of the strap together, leaving a fat leather tube around the base of my cock and balls which were squeezed tight and blossomed out of the end like bloated red fruit. My dickhead and my nuts swelled up bigger than ever, but there was a kind of numb feeling in them. Clay pinched the tip of my dick in his strong fingers: I felt it, but the whole dickhead had lost some of its sensitivity. I still wanted to cum, but now I could actually feel the cumtube squeezed shut and the rising juice held down, building up more and more pressure in my balls with nowhere to go.

The three-inch strap held the whole package out from my crotch. Clay took the mass of meat and balls in both his hands and massaged it firmly. "This strap does two things for us, Teddy. It prevents you from cumming because it compresses your cum chan-

nel, and it also makes it easier for me to get at the whole works when I need to discipline you in the next hour. It makes a better target for our little paddle friend." He brought out the six-inch cock paddle and batted my equipment back and forth, letting the heavy weight of flesh swing and pull heavily on the fat tube of the leather strap.

Instead of making me less horny, though, this torment just made me more desperate for cock, for anything to kiss, or lick, or suck or just rub against.

Clay picked up other objects from the drawer. These were wrist cuffs connected by a chain about eighteen inches long. He put one cuff on my left wrist and then, passing the chain across my butt cheeks behind, snapped the other cuff on my right wrist. Now I could not bring my hands together in front of me. If I reached forward to take hold of something like a cock, the movement ground the chain into my ass or pulled one arm painfully across my back.

"This will help you to concentrate on your mouth training," explained Clay. "I know that the Milk Master showed you some handmilking techniques on the cows today, but for now, and for me, this is a test of your tongue, your lips, your teeth, your cheeks, and your throat. I like mouth play on my dick and balls, and I like for a boy to get me off completely orally. Do you understand that?"

"Yes."

"Yes, Sir," he corrected.

"Yes, Sir," I said.

Clay began to undress until he stood in front of me with his own cock and balls swinging heavily, his penis just starting to thicken and to arch out from his groin.

   ❊ ❊ ❊

Clay's dick and my dick are almost exactly the same size. When I put my fist around the base of my prick, to jack off, about three inches of meat still sticks out beyond it, and if I work it hard and keep my grip tight, the head will swell up almost another inch beyond that. Clay's is the same. It's almost as if we really were related by blood, and had the same genes.

Without squeezing too hard I can get my thumb just barely to meet my forefinger around the shaft of my meat, except on the

head. Both Clay and I have big, fleshy dick crowns that bulge bigger than the shafts below. And we both have deep ridges around the crown. You can wrap a thin rope around the ledge of my dickhead and lead me by it, like a dog on a leash.

We're both cut and the heart-shaped underside of the corona makes a pronounced triangular valley, just deep enough for the point of a probing tongue.

I know all this because by now I've had plenty of chance to look at Clay's meat, twin to mine, close up for long periods of time.

Clay's prick is more mature looking than mine, with bigger, more prominent veins and a head that remains a constant angry purple-red. My penis is still baby-pink and my shaft is smoother and softer. In the precum department, though, I'm the champ. Clay just drips enough to keep his head moist and shiny. My cocklips leak a steady stream of golden goo that runs down my shaft and puddles in my balls.

Both of us have low hanging nuts. I can pull his ball sack down and circle the skin above his two egg-sized testicles with three fingers and my thumb and still have a little loose skin to play with. When I came to The Milk Farm that first time I had fine blond hair on my balls and at the root of my meat. Clay's was darker. Now I am as smooth and soft as velvet all over.

When Clay's dick gets hard it hangs heavily in a swaying droop. Mine gets like a lead pipe standing straight out and bouncing when I walk.

When I began my "tests" on Clay's cock and balls, it was almost like working on my own equipment, we were so much alike.

excerpt from
THE MILK FARM
MEMBERS' HANDBOOK

In-House Channels available on your Hotel TV
(Note: Channels 1–5 are standard commercial stations)

Channel 6
24-hour feed from video monitor cameras mounted in the training sheds of The Milk Farm, including the New Stock Orientation Rooms, and certain sections of the Laboratories. In the training rooms you will see new studcows undergoing milk-supply enhancement exercises—notably machines which supply continuous prostate stimulation while the training cow is hooked up to a mechanical milking sleeve. In video feed from the Laboratories you will see the results of experiments such as the attempt to enlarge milkbag capacity, and to provide naturally flavored cream through special diet and forced feeding.

Channel 7
Constant updates on the current day's milking schedule and on the availability of stock for the following day. A full view of each studcow strapped to his stanchion is given, followed by a closeup examination from face to crotch. Clients who have previously milked certain cows give on-camera evaluations of the flavor and consistency of their juice. Special quirks and likes of individual milkstuds may be listed: for example, "likes a rough, hard pull with lots of teeth" or "shoots extra hard and roars when he cums."

Channel 8
The Punishment Channel: live video feeds from the punishment rooms and stalls in the Staff Compound. Especially popular are the sessions in the "real calf" corral where the teat of a mancow who needs discipline is given to an actual

calf for suckling. Real cow's milk is poured onto the teat to get the calf started and the stud soon begins to realize just what it means to get pulled by a hungry "natural" sucker! Another popular live feed is from the Whipping Room where cows who tend to shoot too quickly are given lengthy penis-whippings to desensitize their cockheads. Occasionally this channel shows the activities in the Security Staff Barracks playroom when Milk Farm guards are given free rein with a Pool Boy or a Room Boy who needs some attitude re-adjustment.

Channel 9
Schedules and news of activities at other Pleasure Corporation branches including the Fuck Corral, the Cocksuck Academy and the SbarM Ranch. Also the daily menu at the Cock and Ball Restaurant in the City. Especially popular are programs from the Wet Room at the SbarM Ranch and the ass-riding competitions from the Fuck Corral. Virgin Suck Nights from the gymnasium locker room at the Cocksuck Academy provide fine entertainment for the connoisseur of "first-time" throat-feeding.

Channel 10
Instructional Channel: master milkers give tips on their techniques, demonstrating on Milk Farm stock. "Tongue-Plugging," the "Gag-Ring Squeeze," and "Full-mouth Gorging" are just three of recent topics.

Channel 11
Special Events Channel: Slave Auctions at the SbarM Ranch; Sports Weekends at the Cocksuck Academy; live feeds from the Dog-Slave School; notices of Sale/Lease offers on stock the Corporation no longer needs.

CHAPTER SIX

Getting Tested

Clay stood naked in front of me, his fists on his hips, his crotch thrust lewdly forward. "Okay, Teddy. This is a three-part exam. Before we go to sleep tonight, you're going to milk me, with your mouth only, three times. Each time I want a different technique. And each time I'll let you know what you did right and what you did wrong. After each milking, I'm going to give you a letter-grade, like A − or B + . You've got to manage at least a B average for the evening, Teddy. My boy is not going to be a mediocre grade C cocksucker. You got that?"

I nodded, a little worried, because at school I tended to be pretty much a C + to B − student.

"The better the overall grade," he continued, "the more rewards you'll get tomorrow. The lower the grade, the more punishments." He stepped forward, grabbed my balls, and twisted. "Did you get that, boy?"

"Yes, Sir," I gasped.

"Okay, then, Let's get this show on the road." He got onto the bed, sitting with his back against the middle of the headboard, but with a pillow under his ass so his crotch jutted forward as he spread his legs wide. "Get down between my legs, Teddy. The position for the first test is on your knees, face to the Vee of my crotch, lips open, tongue out, ready to milk."

I crawled awkwardly onto the bed, not able to support myself with my manacled hands, and knelt down, my face to his dick, which rolled back heavily across his stomach.

He took a small clock-timer from the bedside table drawer and set it. "The first test is a one-hour milking exam, in four parts, each part lasting fifteen minutes," he announced, sounding like the proctor at my SAT exams at the end of school. "First there will be fifteen minutes of tongue work, then fifteen minutes of cheek-filled mouth work on my balls, then lips and teeth on my shaft for fifteen minutes, and a final fifteen minute fullmouth-suck, using

everything you've got.

"Holy cow," I thought, "it *is* like writing college entrance exams—in *cocksucking*!"

"I don't want to feed you until near the end of part four, after I've tested you for about an hour," he warned, "so if I tap your forehead or your cheek at any time with the paddle, you'll know I'm getting too close and want you to back off. If you make me cum before I'm ready, you'll pay for it later. But don't ever lose contact with my meat. I want your mouth in my crotch every second of those sixty minutes."

He pressed a button on the timer. "I'm starting the clock now. The first fifteen minutes is tongue work only, on my shaft and my head. Go to it."

He settled back and widened his thighs even further as I stuck out my tongue and got my first taste of his honeydick.

At first, licking that big poker was a breeze, but I never realized how long fifteen minutes can be when you've only got your tongue to work with. I swabbed his meaty head, flicked back and forth across his pouting cocklips, stuck the tip of my tongue down his cumhole, washed around the edge of the crown, and lapped into the triangle beneath. Then I ran the whole flat surface of my licker up and down the underside of his thick shaft. My tongue began to get tired and I was weary of holding my lips open so it could do its work.

Just when I thought I couldn't go on any longer, Clay said, "That's five minutes gone, Teddy. You've got ten more minutes to show me just how talented that pink puppy tongue of yours can be."

"*Jeez*," I thought, "*only five minutes and I've already run out of tricks!*" I tried to rest a bit by letting my tongue hang loosely from my lower lip, moving my whole head up and down and all around the long shaft. I imagined I was painting that meat with a big, soft brush, and I stroked the paint—my plentiful spit!—onto that pole until it had a satin-smooth finish.

"Ten minutes," he announced, "five more to go."

I tried to look at the timer. The fifteen minutes *had* to be up! It seemed like I had been licking for half an hour. But he jerked my head back in line with his cock. My face was tingling with the stress of keeping my jaw open so that my tongue had free play.

Any time I let my lips close on his dick by mistake, for a little rest, or to swallow, he pulled on my hair and slapped me lightly on the cheek.

"This is the *tongue-test*, boy," he reminded me.

During the last five minutes I went a little bonkers. I corkscrewed my tongue around his fat mushroom head clockwise, then counter-clockwise. I fluttered all up and down the solid stalk like a butterfly. I hardened the tip and stabbed at it. I tried to slap it back and forth using my tired tongue as the paddle. Finally, I just laid the flat surface of my slimy lickmuscle against his cumhole and pressed and lapped, over and over again. This seemed to get him excited, because he slapped my forehead with the little paddle so I would back off. I immediately moved away from the cocklips and trailed slowly down his shaft, at last letting my aching tongue gently fumble at the root, right where the ball sack began.

A little bell pinged on the timer. "Fifteen minutes," he said. "You can lean back and take a little break."

I wanted him to tell me how well I had done, but he just sat there looking at me with a little frown, flexing his dick up and down, as if doing exercises between the rounds of a contest.

Soon he said, "The next fifteen minutes is ball work. Get both my nuts into your mouth and work them. You can spend some time on each one alone, but you've got to show me that you can take care of the whole pouch as well. This is a fullmouth test, Teddy: lips, tongue, the insides of your cheeks, the back of your throat. Don't be afraid to use your teeth, too. I'll let you know if you get too rough for me, but my balls are pretty tough. I think they can take whatever a beginner's mouth like yours can dish out."

I looked down at his nuts. They hung down onto the bed, their weight pulling the skin of his ball sack into two sharp ridges. I couldn't imagine getting them both into my mouth at once.

He set the timer. "Okay, sucker, chow down on those meatballs."

I leaned down to my work once again. It was awkward trying to get my mouth into his crotch, under his dick and into contact with his balls. I tried to remember what he'd done to the Nutboy's eggs earlier, and I remembered seeing some of the customers in the Ball Milking Stall chomping on the cows' milkbags instead of pull-

ing their teats.

I had to turn my face sideways to get my lips down to one of those ripe plums. My nose kept hitting against the heavy stem of his prick, which rolled back and forth across my face as I worked my lips and teeth over the spongy manfruit. I washed it with my tired tongue, pressing it against my cheek-lining, rubbing it against my teeth and gums. I moved across to the other one, never letting my lips leave the skin of his sack. This ball was even bigger and hung a little lower than the first. I kept having to twist my neck painfully to get into position.

After a while, he got restless. "Come on, ballslut, you've played around long enough. Get both those fuckers into your face. Squirrel those big nuts away in your fat cheeks, baby."

Without my hands free to help push them into my mouth, I had to use lots of suction to try to get them both inside. I lodged one nut in my cheek finally and then began to work my lips slowly onto the other one, which kept slipping away, because everything in his crotch was now covered with my slick drool. I could feel him getting angry at my failure. Frantically I used my chin to press the slippery nut against his inner thigh, to keep it from rolling around. Then I inched my lips and teeth down around it, until his whole scrotum was stuffing my mouth cavity. My cheeks were stretched painfully, as if I was trying to blow a trumpet with the mouthpiece stopped up.

Clay put his hands on the distended sides of my face, pressing gently onto his testicles which nestled warmly inside. He squeezed his palms tighter against my ball-filled cheeks, then rotated my whole head slowly in circles, letting his nuts move in my mouth at will. He rubbed the lower side of his pliant, arching penis against my nose. I could feel sticky fucklube coating my forehead.

He bent his semi-hard dick down and painted my eyelids shut with the gooey juice seeping from its tip. I started to pull away, dragging his nutsack away from his body, his balls still firmly bulging in my cheeks. He seemed to like that, because he groaned and murmured, "Oh, yeah, Teddy, pull those fuckers, pull 'em hard."

I tugged harder and waggled my head back and forth like a dog pulling on a piece of meat held by his master. His prong got iron hard again and stood straight up from his pubic patch, jerking and straining. He slapped my forehead sharply with the paddle, and

I knew I had almost made him cum. Remembering what he had said about punishment if this happened too soon, I pushed one ball out of my mouth with my tongue, then let the other one pop out, and started licking the little seam of flesh on the sack separating those two wet beauties, just to cool him off.

The bell pinged. "That's fifteen minutes, kid," he sighed. "Take a breather."

I wanted desperately to know how I was doing. Was I pleasing him enough to get a good mark and to avoid whatever punishment a C grade cocksucker deserved? I leaned back and tried to ease the ache in my shoulders and neck from the corkscrew contortions of nutsucking, without hands to help me. Clay kept his eyes closed and breathed deeply, a tiny smile hovering at his lips. His dick began to fall back into its malleable state, lolling wetly against his belly. His balls glistened with my saliva, the fine ballhairs plastered against the red flesh. His inner thighs gleamed with my slobber.

After a few minutes, he opened his eyes and stared at me. I couldn't read his expression. It might have been approval and it might have been disappointment.

"It's lip time, Teddyboy," he began. "You've got fifteen minutes to show me what those pretty young smackers can do on my dick. You can use your teeth, too. I won't penalize you for a little light nibbling, but I want to see how good you are at covering those white milkteeth with your lips. I want to feel you gum that meat, and remember, my shaft has got a top and a bottom and two sides. It's got a head with a rim and a triangle of loose skin beneath. It's got a cumhole and two cumlips. And it's got a root down in my crotch. That root goes back between my legs almost to my asshole. I want your lips on every square inch of that package. And I want to feel your pulling power on my teat. I want a solid, full-length jackoff with those virgin boylips. Get to it."

He set the timer as I crouched into position, once again praying at the altar of his cock and balls, ready to make my daddy's milkteat feel good enough to feed me.

For the next quarter of an hour I did something, but I'm not sure what exactly. My back muscles were so tired from the strain of serving hunched in his groin, and jaw so stiff from the effort of holding my mouth open, that I just worked mindlessly, like a milking machine. But I must have been doing something right, because

he slapped my cheek several times with the paddle during the lip test to show that I was getting him close to shooting. Each time I quickly stopped what I was doing, forced my jaw open even wider, so my lips lost contact with his flesh, and exhaled steamy breath on that throbbing meat until I felt his climax point begin to recede.

When the fifteen minutes were up, he pushed my face roughly off his dick, gasping, "Back off, fucker. You're finished with this part of your exam."

I sat back on my heels, stretching my shoulders to get out the kinks, moving my cuffed hands as much as I could to loosen up. I wondered what the fourth part of this first test could possibly be. I'd used every part of my mouth I could think of, unless he was going to count my throat as part of my mouth equipment. I hadn't had a throat test yet, and that worried me because my practice sessions in The Milking Barn hadn't really prepared me for anything too big going too deep.

Clay sat up straighter on the bed. He lit a cigarette and after a couple of drags on it began speaking. "Before we go on to part four of this first test—before I let you take your first load of daddymilk, Teddy—I'm going to give you a little review of what's been wrong with your performance so far. Maybe you can correct some of your mistakes during the next part and redeem your grade, which right now is sitting at about a D + ."

"*Dee-plus!!!*" I was shocked. I had worked my chops until I thought my tongue would fall out and my lips would shrivel up. He'd had to warn me off several times because I almost made him cum. And now he said it was worth a D + ! I wanted to tell him that his grading system sucked worse than I did. But I thought twice about that considering I was locked into wrist straps and had my nuts and dick squeezed down in a three-inch leather strap.

"Kneel down on the floor at the foot of the bed," he ordered. He crawled down to the foot as well and sat there with his thighs spread wide so his cock and balls hung in front of my face. "Move your head right into my crotch, Teddy. I want you to concentrate on your daddy's milkteat and his milkbags while he tells you what's wrong with your milking technique."

I crouched down a little more on my haunches so my face was only an inch from that warm flesh. He put his hand on the back

of my neck and pulled me firmly against his penis, so my nose and mouth were pressed against it and my chin nestled into his low hanging testicles.

"First," he said, "your tongue work is lousy. You've got no concentration. It's just a shitty little bit of this and a shitty little bit of that. It's sissy sucking. When you lick the shaft, use the whole flat surface of your licker right to its root at the back of your mouth. Start deep in my crotch, down in the crotch hair and take long, unbroken licks to the very tip. Then go back and do the same thing again, and again. Do it fifty times, even a hundred. A dedicated licker knows that repetition is the key. And when you work the tip of your tongue into my cumhole, don't just dip into it like a fairyboy. Plunge that hard point down into that tubehole and use it like a little spoon to dig around in there. Excavate that fucker. Finally, your lapping on my dickhead was pathetic. A man wants the big head on the end of his prick swabbed down. Treat it like a cow slavering on a saltlick. The whole tongue, on the whole head, covering it like a foreskin, moving constantly, every inch of head in hot, slurpy contact with every inch of tongue—that's the goal. Have you got that?"

"Yes," I answered, abashed at this list of my failings.

"Yes, *what*?"

"Yes, *Sir*!"

But he wasn't finished. "Your ball sucking is just average. You got both nuts in your cheeks, but I had to use my own hands to get any pressure on them. Your cheeks have got to have suction power. You've got to be able to squeeze those bags like you were playing an accordion. And, again, your tonguing was dim. Just because your mouth is full of mannuts doesn't mean that your licker gets to rest. Find that line between the two balls on the nut sack and work up and down on it. And you didn't even think to use your teeth to nip the loose skin at the base of my nuts. A good nuteater will come away with ball hairs between his teeth, because he's used his molars to nibble and lovebite all over that loose pouch."

He pressed my face harder into his groin. "Are you listening, Teddy?"

'Yes, Sir," I answered in a muffled voice that sounded like I had a bad cold, because my nose was mashed flat against the broad

underside of his rising cock.

"And last, your lip work was all over the place." The list of my faults would never end! "There was no dedication in it, no commitment, no CONCENTRATION! You pull like a girl. A man wants his prick *vacuumed* into those lips. He wants to feel as if those lips are going to pull his fuckstalk right out at the root. And you've got to get a lot of practice on stretching your lips down and over your choppers. You've got to cover those teeth so it feels to the guy like you're sucking him with your gums only, as if your teeth had all been pulled out."

I had a sudden vision of myself with a toothless, gummy grin, grinding away at a succession of dicks thrust into my maw. Clay pulled my hair back in his fist, tilting my face up to look into his hard eyes.

"But the main problem, Teddy, is that you just don't concentrate. You're just dicking around down there, playing at milking, not really going to it with your whole heart and mind. It's a mental problem, Teddy. You're in a man's crotch for one reason: to please him and to get his milk. Nothing else matters and your own feelings don't exist. Is that clear?"

"Yes, Sir."

"So, what are you going to do, Teddy?"

"I'm going to concentrate, Sir."

"Concentrate on what, Teddy?"

"I'm going to concentrate on my sucking, Sir."

"Good boy." He let go of my head and stubbed his cigarette out in the ashtray he'd brought down beside him. "Now we come to part four of this first test. I'm going to give you fifteen minutes to pop my load using everything you've learned so far. Tongue, lips, teeth, cheeks—the full treatment on cock and balls and all around in my crotch. This is where we see if you've got any imagination, Teddy. Can you put it all together and do a professional cocksucking job?

"Yes, Sir, I'll try my best," I promised.

"I'm going to give you a few minutes to get your head straight. Think about how you can please me. Start concentrating on getting my milk." He got back into his position on the bed. I stayed where I was with my eyes closed, going over what he had said, trying to imagine what I could do to get his cream, trying to "put it

all together," as he had described.

At last I crawled into my familiar position between his thighs and said, meekly, "I'm ready, Sir."

He started the timer and spread his legs as far as they would go to give me the fullest access possible. I leaned my face down, opened my lips, took a deep breath, stuck out my tongue, and began to milk him.

After a few minutes he started to make a deep-pitched sound in his throat on every out-breath. Then, he began mumbling to himself. Gradually I began to pick out words and phrases as I slaved away on his meat.

"Oh yes," he breathed, over and over. "Milk me, milk me," he intoned again and again. Then, goading me, "Come on, suckboy, eat me good. Come on, baby, suck your teat." Finally he began threatening me, promising me, "Daddy's gonna feed you now, milkboy. Daddy's gonna fill your little boymouth. Keep milkin'! Keep milkin' that dick, you little spermsucker. You're gonna get fed!!"

He pulled my head back so my mouth was just on the crown of his trembling dick. He was groaning and thrashing around on the bed. In the midst of his ecstasy he gasped out, "Don't swallow it, baby! Don't swallow! Just hold it in your mouth!"

Then, it was all there! Hot lava on my tongue, in my cheeks, coating my teeth, trying to spurt down my throat as I closed it off so as not to swallow. The gushing cream piled up, backed up, and began to fill my cheeks as full as his balls had. Little spurts began to squeeze out at the corners of my lips, but I held on as he pumped his warm jism into my face.

Little by little, after a series of decreasing jerks and spasms, his tube stopped spewing and just floated in the warm syrup of cum and spit which filled my oral cavity. I wanted to swallow, but I didn't dare. I gagged, and some of his milk came out of my nose, dripping down on his softening shaft.

He caressed my hair with his hand, still crooning deep in his throat, "Nice baby . . . good suckbaby . . . sweet milkboy."

After a pause, while I whined and grunted, trying to keep the mass of liquid in my mouth without swallowing, he put his palms on the sides of my face and looked down into my eyes.

"I'm going to pull out now, Teddy, and when I do I want you

to let my cum dribble slowly out of your lips, all over my cock and balls. Let it drip into my crotch hair and down my thighs into the sweaty patch beneath my nuts. And when it's all dribbled out, take your face and rub all over my crotch. I'll help you. We'll rub that sweet mug all through that man-paste and get your whole face plastered with it. My crotch and your face, Teddy, glued together with your first load of daddy's sticky cream."

I did as he said. And he directed me with his big hands, moving my head all over his groin, pressing me down deep, almost to his asshole, until the cum was so sticky that it gave a little sucking sound when my cheek moved off his thigh. Then he leaned down and released the wrist cuffs.

"There, now," he said, "you can lie on your side and snuggle into the Vee of my legs. Take my milkteat back in your mouth and just let it soak there for a while. Just suckle me softly while we rest and get ready for the next test."

I nursed at his soft dick and brought my freed hands up to cup his sticky balls. He shifted his thighs closer together and encased me in warm, sweaty flesh.

"And, Teddy, you made a lot of improvement after my criticism. That was a solid B – fuck. There are still some problems, but we're going to try to solve them during the rest of the evening."

Bee-minus!!! Again I was shocked. After all that groaning and thrashing, after all that sweet-talk—"*Good baby! . . . Nice baby! . . . Eat me, baby!*"—after that quart of cream he shot, he was giving me a B – ?! It wasn't fair. Just what did a guy have to do to get an A?!

We rested about twenty minutes, my eyes glaring at him because of my shitty B – grade, his soft dick soaking in my tired mouth, leaking dribbles of cum, which I finally got to swallow.

He turned on the TV while we lay there and watched the channel that showed which cows would be in The Milking Barn stalls the next day. The screen gave a full view of each mancow strapped into his stall and then the camera examined each stud in detail. Special features were noted by the Milk Master, such as "leaks a nut-flavored precum" or "likes rough ball-handling." Then he switched channels to a live-feed from The Fuck Corral at the SbarM Ranch where men were tied over sawhorses getting rough-fucked by studs with horsedicks. Finally he turned off the TV and

pulled my head off his cock, holding me up by my hair.

"It's time for test number two, suckleboy. This one is very simple. It's a test of whether or not you listened to everything I told you was wrong with your technique in test number one. You remember I gave you an evaluation of your sucking before the last part?"

I nodded sullenly, still angry about my poor grade on test one.

"What did I say about your licking, Teddy?" he quizzed.

"You said it was lousy."

"Right! And do you remember why it was lousy, Teddy?"

"Yes, it's because—" He cut short my answer by stuffing his cock back into my mouth and pressing my head down so it slithered into my throat.

"I do want to hear your answers, Teddy, but I think you'll concentrate on them even more with this in your mouth."

How the fuck was I supposed to answer with a mouthful of prick?!

"So, Teddy, why is your tongue work lousy?"

I tried to answer, "*You said it was a little bit of this and a little bit of that,*" but it came out as "ooh eh ah ih aw ay i'h'le ih uh iss ah ay i'h'le ih uh ah."

"No, no," he complained, "you've got to do better than that. You see this test has two purposes. I want to see if you remember the cocksucking faults I pointed out to you, and, just so we don't waste time, I want you to learn to talk clearly with your mouth full, because the more clearly you try to talk around my prick, the more pleasure I'm going to get from all that tongue and lip and jaw movement. And maybe, if you speak really clearly, with nice sharp consonants and long, wet vowels, I'll get so excited that I'll feed you again. How would that be, Teddy?"

"Ooh ay, eye ess" ("*Okay, I guess*"), I said!

"I didn't understand that, Teddy. Say it again," he prompted.

I tried. "*Oh*" (that wasn't so hard—I just made a circle of my lips around the dick-shaft and said it). The "*kay*" of "okay" was a problem. To make the letter *K* I had to bite down lightly on his prick. I wasn't sure that was a good idea, but I did it anyway.

"I didn't get that last bit, Teddy, say it again."

"*Oh—KAY,*" I said, and bit down hard to make the *K* sound.

"Okay? Is that what you said?" he asked. "Now see, that wasn't

so bad, and I got a nice hot breath of air on your 'Oh' and a great little chew-thrill on your 'kay.'" He pulled his dick out a little farther so that my lips and tongue could work nearer the head. "So, once again. Tell me what's wrong with your tongue work."

I knew the answer: "*When I lick the shaft I have to use the whole surface of my tongue.*" That's what he had told me. But getting it out clearly, so he could understand it, with his swelling penis in my mouth was another matter.

The "*WH*" of "when" was easy, but the *N* could only be made clearly by putting my tongue against the head of his dick and pressing off hard against it. He seemed to like all the spit that was involved in that move. "Lick" was another word he liked a lot. The *L* took a tongue swab on his tender frenulum and the *K* gave his pole another bite. The *F* and *T* of "shaft" brought both my lips and tongue into play. He had me repeat "*sha-F-T*" until it was crystal clear. And the word "surface" sent him into little spasms with its combination of licks and lip-presses and hot breath.

So it went, through the whole litany of errors. He, asking questions. Me, giving cock-mouthed answers. He, saying he couldn't understand. Me, working my mouth around that invading monster to make my replies clear, while giving him a unique blow job.

His dick got harder and harder and my "penis-pronunciation" got muddier and muddier as my tongue had less room to maneuver and my lips were stretched so taut that pressing them tighter was a struggle.

The end came as he put me through my paces on the word "concentrate":

C (bite hard on the shaft)
ON (wet, forward lick of tongue on underpart of head)
C (bite again)
EN (lick again)
TRA (tip of tongue pushed off cumhole)
TE (repeat tongue push-off).
C-bite-ON-lick-C-bite-EN-lick-TRA-push-Te-push.
bite, lick, bite, lick, push, push
bitelickbitelickpushpush
again, and again, and again!

He made me "say" it fifty times as he began to breathe faster and faster, until finally he groaned, "Fuck this! It's time to cream you."

And he rolled over on his stomach, taking me with him, attached at the mouth to his hard cock. He lay heavily on my face and thrust his meat forcefully down my throat. Long, grinding thrusts, up and down into my gullet. I started to gag and slobber, making wet sounds. He kept saying, "That's right, baby, talk to me. Talk to daddy's dick."

Then he went rigid, pushing his steel-pipe down my neck, and I felt hot splashings of cum spurt against the sensitive lining of my throat. I couldn't taste it. I could only sense its warmth and feel the jerks of the fleshtube it was coming from against my tonsils. The more I gagged, the more he shot, as if the gagging itself were squeezing out his juice.

At last he slumped down, smothering my whole face with his sweaty crotch, his balls draped over my chin, my nose buried in his pubic hair. I thought I was going to suffocate. I pushed at his thighs with my hands and tried to work his cock out of my throat by twisting my head sideways. This only seemed to excite him again and he ground his spent meat into my face, moving his hips in small circles, reaming out my throat, drilling down with his semi-hard member. More warm liquid oozed down my gullet. His movement had freed my nose, so I was able to breathe again.

"Let me hear it again, Teddy. One more time—the magic word."

"*Con-cen-trate*," I said wetly around his soft meat.

bite—lick—bite—lick—push—push

"Oh, yeah," he sighed, as he rolled off me, "you're a sweet-talker, Teddyboy. That was definitely a B performance. Nice work, kid."

I couldn't believe my cum-soaked ears. A *Bee performance?!* One lousy step up from the B – , for the first test? After I had practically dislocated my jaw, learning to talk around a massive dick?

I decided it was time for a Grade Appeal!

excerpt from
THE MILK FARM
MEMBERS' HANDBOOK

Nighttime Hotel Room Services

(available 9:00 p.m. to 9:00 a.m.)

Exercise Boy. A well-muscled young man will be delivered bound to your room for a maximum 30 minutes of light abuse. A toybox is included in the Service. (Time extensions may be arranged with the Front Desk.) Clients who have never played with an Exercise Boy before need not worry about knowing what to do. The Boys are trained to provide indirect guidance: for example, "Please Sir, don't put those big clips on my tits . . . please Sir, don't pull on my tit clips when you chew on my balls . . . please Sir, don't bite my tits the second you pull the clips off."

Trainer. A 30-minute work-out from head to toe. The Milk Farm Trainers use lightweight penis-whips only, and guarantee to leave no permanent marks on any part of your body. Any Client who orders a Trainer to his room must be willing to let this specially equipped expert take charge and exercise his skills. All our Trainers prefer to work with bound subjects, so Clients must expect to be cuffed hand and foot during the session. It is up to the discretion of each Trainer whether he will allow the Client to climax and whether the Client will be allowed mouth or ass contact with the Trainer's cock and balls. Clients whose cries are likely to disturb neighboring rooms can expect to be fitted with ball-gags. "Long Session" Trainers are also available.

Night Nurser. A milkteat to suckle as you sleep. You crawl between fresh-hay smelling sheets and prop your head up

on a nice firm pillow. You have taken a light sedative, found in the bedside drawer, so you feel cozy and drowsy, ready for your warm milk. Then, in comes a big gentle milkbull, all snowy white muscles, with a swollen semi-soft teat. He stands beside the head of your bed, puts one knee up on the bed beside you and lowers that juicy tube right into your yawning mouth. You don't have to do a thing except nuzzle. The milkbull gentles that milk teat up and down in your throat until you're ready to drop off to sleep, and just before you lose consciousness, he pours a big mouthful of warm white cream down into your throat. Then, off you go with that soft suckletube between your lips. In the morning when you wake, he'll be sitting lightly on your chest with his massive milk-filled balls draped over your mouth, his fat cock lying on your cheek, dribbling a little early morning precum onto your face. All you have to do is open your lips, stick out your tongue, and lazily go to work for your first drink of the day. Some Night Nursers are especially trained to service you all night if you want. They will keep your mouthhole stuffed with milkmeat for several hours while you doze and they will cum two or three times as you grind your teeth and suckle that foreskin all night long. May be combined with Pillow Boy Service.

Pillow Boy. Rest your head on a soft flesh pillow: the ass, stomach, chest, back or crotch of a soft-skinned young man. May be combined with Morning Juice Service.

Morning Juicer. Leave a time-call. The Juicer will wake you in his special way, delivering either fresh orange piss or a light cream eye-opener directly into your mouth.

CHAPTER SEVEN

The Final Exam

We were lying side by side on the bed now, and Clay was mellowing out after his second shoot, so I decided it was a good time to make my bid for a fairer grading system.

"Uh, Clay . . ." I began.

"Yes, Teddy?"

"Uh, I was wondering about the grade, Clay."

"What about it?" His voice was cold now.

"Well, I was just wondering why it was so low."

"What's low about a B, Teddy?" He was not at all sympathetic. "A B is a very good mark."

"I know," I pressed on, foolishly, "but I was just wondering why it wasn't higher, you know, because I thought I was doing pretty good."

"Well, I'll tell you, Teddy"—his voice had taken on a nasty quality—"your diction is still sloppy. Your consonants have no real bite and your Tees—You've got to push off hard against that dicktip with your tongue to make a good Tee sound. Then let's take a word like 'balls.' Your lips were too slack on that one. You've got to press hard to get the Bee sound, and then the double Ell needs a long wet lick from far down the shaft right up to the tip, to be clear. And you just don't seem to understand how to make a decent Ess sound at all."

This was bad! Why had I been so dumb as to question his judgment?

"Then you forgot a couple of things I had pointed out about your milking performance," he went on relentlessly. "For example, you didn't mention using your teeth to nip at the hairs on my nut sack."

"*Shit,*" I thought, "*now I'm losing points because I forgot to eat the fucking hairs on his balls!*"

"I don't know, Teddy. I thought a B was more than generous considering what an unsatisfactory job you did on my meat, but

now I'm starting to think I should re-evaluate—maybe take it down to a C."

I could see that this was only going to get my balls into more trouble. "No, no," I hurried, "I understand you, Clay—uh, Sir—I see my problems now. Thanks for giving me the B. I know I probably don't deserve it." I got down and licked at the soft head of his dick, like a dog trying to make it up with his angry master.

"That's the way, kid," he approved. "Take it like a man."

He let me nuzzle his crotch for a few minutes, then gave me a slap on the butt. "Now, then, let's take a refreshment break before test number three. What do you say?"

"Yes, Sir," I answered eagerly. "I feel like I need one."

"First, though, I've got to take a piss. How would you like to be my piss puppy?"

"I guess that would be okay," I said, a little worried about what being a "piss puppy" involved.

He stood up by the side of the bed, his meat, even in its soft state a potent swinging club. "Come over here beside me, on your knees. . . . Now take the shaft of my dick in your lips, so you're holding it like a dog holds a bone, right in the middle."

I took a good mouth grip on his "bone."

"Now we'll walk into the bathroom," he directed, "and you'll crawl along beside me, holding my big milkbone in your mouth."

He walked slowly as I crabbed sideways trying to keep his prong in my lips. At the toilet, he stood, straddling the bowl, me at the side, meat still in my mouth. "Now angle your head to point my dickhead down toward the water, Teddy, and just hold it." After a moment, beneath the soft skin my lips were gripping, I felt his warm piss begin to flow through the shaft as it streamed into the toilet bowl. Since his hands were free, he used them to pinch and pull lightly at his own tits as he pissed. When he was through, he pulled my head back off the shaft, took his dick in hand and casually wiped the last dribbles of warm liquid across my half-opened lips. Then we went back into the bedroom, my strapped cock and balls still flopping back and forth against my thighs as I crawled behind him.

"How about a drink, Teddy? Shall we see what the evening Room Service Cocktail is?"

"Yeah," I agreed readily. "I'm kind of thirsty."

"You young milkpuppies just can't get enough to drink, can you?" he laughed. "Two big loads of cream tonight and you're still thirsty! Well, don't forget, there's another big mouthful of hot milk for you to swallow if you pass the third test. But we'll order something now, anyway." He let me call Room Service to find out what the night's Special was. The man on the Room Service phone said that the evening drink was a Milk Farm Black Russian. At Clay's direction I told them to send the Waiter right up to room 27.

While we waited, he had me sit on his lap in the big easy chair, and he cuddled my nuts while he frenched my mouth with long, wet, tongue-probing kisses. For him it seemed quite natural, but for me it was mind-blowing. I had never been kissed by a man. In fact I'd hardly ever been kissed by anybody! And certainly not with an aggressive muscular tongue reaming out every corner of my mouth. If the Room Waiter hadn't knocked on the door I'd have cum buckets in spite of the big strap squeezing my cumtube shut.

The same cocktail server who had given us our "dry" martini that afternoon appeared with his cart, only this time he had in tow, attached to the cart by a chain through a ring in one of his tits, a big black guy dressed in nothing except wrist straps and a black leather belt. His cock was a billy-club of shiny brown flesh.

The Milk Farm Black Russian, he said, was going to be a mixture of vodka and Kahlua mixed over ice and poured into a big frosted pitcher, followed by a dollop of cream from the beautiful chocolate dick. As the black stud moved up to milk his prong into the pitcher, the Waiter, who had seen how my dick and balls were tied up, and who probably had noticed that my face was cum-sticky and my lips suck-puffy, suggested to Clay, "Perhaps your boy would like to pull the cream for your drink."

"Good idea!" Clay said enthusiastically. "I think he's up to that. Teddy, get down there and suck out the special ingredient for our Black Russians."

I knelt at the massive bronze log and slowly worked my lips over its bulging purple head. I could only manage to get half-way up that big crown, but I licked the slit and tried to suck in my cheeks hard. The guy was apparently well-primed because within minutes he grunted and pulled out, grabbing his cock and holding it over the pitcher of vodka and Kahlua in the Waiter's hands. It oozed

out, making a thick scum on the surface of the deep brown mixture, floating like whipped cream on top of iced coffee. The Waiter then seized the long chocolate tube firmly and used it as a stirrer to mix in the cream. The cold liquid caused the steely dick to soften, and the Waiter whipped it like a whisk to froth the drink up. Then he poured each of us a glass and handed them out.

I tasted it: there was the lush chocolate savor of Kahlua, which I'd had before, the powerful rush of the smooth vodka, and another mouth-watering tang from the man cream. It made you want to drink it all down in one big gulp.

"That's a great drink!" Clay said, licking his lips.

"Thank you, Sir," the Waiter replied. "Our special Breakfast Cocktail tomorrow morning is a Bollinger's Champagne Cocktail with a dash of Milk Farm "bitters" served right at your bedside, if you're interested."

"Sounds good," said Clay, "we'll let you know."

While this was going on the big black creamcow sidled over to me, stretching his tow-chain taut, and began to thrust his hefty dick against my arm, as if he wanted me to do something with it.

"NO!" the Waiter said sharply. "Back off!" He looked at me as he pulled the guy back to the cart by his tit-chain. "He just wants you to milk him again. He liked your mouth the first time. But he's got to give at least three more servings tonight, so we can't let him use it on some little suckboy." He turned and looked at Clay. "No offense, Sir."

"Sure, we understand. Besides the little suckboy has some more service of his own to give tonight."

They left and Clay sat down again in the easy chair and pulled me down onto his lap. We'd take a sip of the Black Russians and then mingle the sweet drinks together in long sloppy kisses. I felt his cock begin to swell up into my ass-crack and I started to wonder just what the third test was going to be. It seemed like I'd had a cock or a pair of balls in my mouth all day. I couldn't imagine how many more tricks I could play with my tongue. Surprisingly, though, I hadn't got to drink all that much milk! Especially during the first two tests. I'd only just barely tasted Clay's first load because I'd had to let it dribble out to coat his crotch and my face. I still felt the stiff mask of dried sperm on my cheeks and forehead, although Clay had begun to wash some of it off with his rough

tongue as his kisses started to wander farther and farther from my lips. And the second load had shot so far down into my throat that it by-passed my tastebuds. So, although I had a tired mouth, I still wanted some manmilk to top off my first day as a cocksucker. I was getting used to the name. It suited me.

My reverie was broken as Clay got up, leaving me to sink into the chair alone. He went to the telephone to talk to the Room Service desk again.

"This is Mr. Brock in Room 27. Is the Trainer I ordered for this evening available yet? . . . Good. Have him come up."

He came back and poured another Black Russian into my empty glass. I slugged it back into my aching throat. I started to feel light-headed and dizzy. Clay reached into the bedside table drawer and pulled out a cigarette. He lit up, and sat down in the other chair, facing me. Soon the good smell of prime weed came to me, and I realized it wasn't his usual brand of cigarette, it was a joint! Clay was smoking pot, right in front of me! Considering that he'd been sticking his big peter down my throat for a couple of hours, I don't know how I could still be shocked by the sight of him with a joint in his mouth, but I was.

Then he passed it over to me, cool as a cucumber, and told me to take a hit. Stunned, I inhaled a lungful of the potent smoke and held it. Then, after exhaling, I guzzled another slurp of the brown dynamite in my glass. I offered the joint back to him, but he told me to keep it and hit it hard.

"I want you as high as you can get for the next test, because it'll be a lot more fun if you're flying."

"What's the next test going to be, Dad?" I asked, finally daring to call him by the name I'd always wanted to.

He grinned and said, "It's your final exam. The biggest test of your powers of CON-CEN-TRA-TION," he leered, flicking his tongue between his lips, "and we both know that's what you need to work on most, don't we?"

I giggled as I finished off the roach. I stood up and waggled my hips, making my heavy, leather-strapped meat and potatoes flop around at my crotch. "I could con-cen-tra-te a lot better if I had someone to take care of this for me," I taunted, boldly.

"Oh, we're going to take care of that," he snickered, "don't worry. But before you get off, you've got to earn your pleasures."

He held up his dripping, semi-hard prick and primed it with slow jacks up and down the shaft. "You've got to focus on *this* and strip my milk for me one more time tonight."

With a woozy lurch I stumbled down to my knees between his legs. "Okay, Sir," I slurred, "if that's what it takes, I'm ready." I swigged down the last of the Black Russian and boozily nuzzled my nose into the warm nest where his cock shaft met his heavy nuts. My sloppy tongue began to slurp at those big orbs and I rubbed my forehead back and forth against the huge erector muscle that ran like a pipeline up the underside of his shaft. I thought I was all ready for my third load of daddy milk. But I was wrong.

There was a knock at the door. As he got up to answer it, I fell forward and sprawled with my face into the cushion where the warm, funky imprint of his ass enveloped me.

"Come in," I heard him say. "I'm Clay, and that boyslut over there with his head buried in the seat of the chair is Teddy."

Another voice, deep and cold, said, "I'm Ed. I've brought my training equipment for an open-ended session. Is Teddy the subject?"

"Yeah," Clay replied. "He's milked me twice this evening, but I want him to take my load a third time. He's new to sucking, and I'm testing him to see if he's a natural cocklicker."

I tried to push myself up into a sitting position, because I wanted to hear this clearly.

"So far," Clay continued, "he's not doing so hot. It's mainly a problem of concentration. Do you think you can help him focus on his duty?"

"Let's see what we've got to work with," the deep voice rumbled.

I felt two strong hands grip my arms and lift me to my feet. I swayed a little and smiled drunkenly at a thin, sinewy man with short-cropped black hair and mean eyes. My eyes trailed down to his leather vest, open over a hard, lean chest, and to the fat pouch in his black leather jockstrap, finally coming to rest on his big black boots. I felt a firm hand palm my cockhead and grind it down against my balls, still squeezed up against my dick by the tight strap. Then his blunt fingers crawled over those balls, probing and pulling. He smacked the whole dangling mass of strapped flesh with the back of his hand.

"OW!" I yelled, and tried to pull away.

Another pair of hands, Clay's, seized me from behind and held me still.

"We'll want to get this strap off his works. I'll need freedom down there. He's got nice equipment. I'll want full access to it."

"That's okay," Brock said, "as long as he doesn't shoot. I'm saving his milk for a special graduation treat. I've strapped him up to keep him from accidentally popping, and I cuffed his hands for the first two milkings, because I want him trained as a mouth-puller only."

"I guarantee you I can keep him from cumming," the Trainer said dryly. With that, he reached down and unsnapped the wide leather band that had been constricting the shaft of my dick and the upper skin of my ballbag. It felt great to have my nuts and prick hang free again. The Trainer massaged them to get them to move easily between my legs.

"Shall we cuff him again?" asked Clay.

"Well, that depends. Are you going to throat-fuck him from above or do you want him kneeling between your legs?"

"I want him doing all the work this time," Clay said. "That's the whole point of this last milking. I've already reamed his gullet. This time I want every ounce of his energy concentrated on getting me off. I'm just going to lay back and watch him eat."

"Then, I think we'll leave his hands free. He'll need to support himself on the bed while he mouths you."

They were talking about me as if I was a dumb animal they were going to put through obedience school. But somehow, in my high state, with the liquor and the pot still making me soar, I didn't care.

"Get comfortable on the bed," the Trainer told Clay, who climbed back up against the headboard, thighs spread, thick meat arching out over pendulous balls which draped onto the sheet. Then the Trainer grabbed me by the nuts and led me over to the foot of the bed facing that steamy crotch. "Crawl up there on your hands and knees, boy," he ordered, giving my ass a hard swack with his open hand.

I swayed a little as I moved into the familiar position. The last time I'd gotten into this pose I'd had my meat squeezed tight and my hands cuffed to my sides. Now, with my balls swinging freely between my legs, and my hands to support me on either side of

Clay's muscular thighs, I thought it was going to be a piece of cake!

"Spread your legs wider, boy," the Trainer ordered.

I moved my knees apart a little more.

"I said *wider*, pussyface," he snarled, jerking my legs so wide I thought my ass would split. Now I saw why I needed to have my hands free to support my upper body, as my head fell naturally into the sweaty groin facing me.

"I think we'd better fix the spread of these legs permanently for our little session," the Trainer said. I heard him zip open the big black gym bag he'd brought with him. There was a metallic, clanking sound. I looked back through my spread thighs, upside down, to see him attach a fleece-lined cuff around each leg just above the knee. Connecting these cuffs was a solid iron rod about three feet wide which locked my thighs into a gaping, immovable opening. Hanging down in that space, in front of the Trainer's hands and torso, I saw my dick and balls, now totally at his mercy. When Clay saw what Ed was doing to me, his meat lifted heavily into the air and grazed my cheek which was hovering over it.

"Now, Teddy," began the Trainer, "I'm going to help you concentrate on milking your daddy's teat. First get your mouth around that big purple head and start tonguing it, the way I'm sure he's taught you."

I did as he told me, savoring the velvet feel of the moist, heart-shaped glans. Just when I was really getting in my tongue work— or thought I was— *WHACK!*—across my ass there was a searing flash of pain. I jerked away from the dick in my mouth and tried to look back to see what the Trainer was beating me with. I caught a glimpse of a wide wooden paddle of the kind used in my high school athletic Letter Club initiations. But I didn't get to look long, because the Trainer reached under and grabbed my dangling nuts so tight I thought they'd pop open. I cried out, but my cry was cut off in midflight by Clay's fist in my hair jerking my open mouth back onto his dickhead.

"Don't look back here, cuntface," the Trainer shouted. "What's going on back here has one purpose—to CONCENTRATE your mind on your work up there. Every smack on this boyass is to remind you that you've got one reason for living right now—to get the hot milk from your daddy's juicy teat."

Then he whacked me again with the paddle. I yelped around

the dick in my mouth and began to lick frantically all over the head. I had gotten the message immediately: the punishment would continue until I managed to suck the juice out of that tube in my face for the third time that evening.

More blows followed, each one driving me to greater efforts. Then, just when I thought I was beginning to have some effect on him, Clay said, "I think it's going to take something a little nastier than that paddle. This lazylicker is still just playing around down there in my crotch. He's just not concentrating yet."

"Jesus, not concentrating!" My whole being was centered, I thought, in my tongue whipping around that head. But I soon found out that I hadn't even begun to learn the meaning of *concentrated* milking!

The paddle blows stopped. "Let's move on to the crop, then," the Trainer suggested. "Maybe a few quick snaps on that pretty pink asshole will wake him up."

"No," Clay said, "we're saving his asshole for another visit. First we want to get his mouthhole in prime shape. Don't take his cherry with a riding crop."

"Well, whatever you say, Mr. Brock, but I've got to tell you that about a dozen quick flicks of this stinger on that rosebud will do wonders with his mouth. He'll open up real quick, if you'll just let me give his asshole a whipping. I promise not to ruin any fun you've got planned for it later."

"Oh, what the hell! Go ahead," offered Clay, "give him a few cracks. Just don't spoil him."

At that, I felt a funny kind of tickling, right in my asscrack where my hole was. I looked back through my legs again, and got a hard tug of my head back into his groin by Clay who growled, "I'm going to tie your mouth down on this dick with a neckrope if you don't keep your tongue working on my meat. You don't need to see what he's doing. You'll feel it soon enough."

The tickling became a light tapping, right on my asshole pucker. I was nervous but excited because no one had ever played around with my ass before. My dick started to swell up big. I almost forgot what I was doing with my tongue as I gave in to the little tapping caresses on my tender hole.

Then the tapping got harder, sharper, and became quick popping snaps of the leather tongue of the crop against my wrinkled

hole. I yelled at every zap, and the yells widened my mouth, so the dick I was sucking went in deeper.

"Now he's getting with the program," Clay said contentedly. "His throat is opening up very nicely."

"I'd like to give him about three maximum shots," the Trainer said, "just to see if he's *really* loosening up."

"Do it," Clay agreed eagerly.

There was a short pause. Then I heard a *WHOOOSH!* as the crop came down fast from a long distance above and stung my hole like a red hot poker. I screamed and lunged forward, impaling my throat on Clay's cock. The two following blows were even harder, and I found myself burrowing my nose and forehead into his pubic hair and his stomach as if I wanted to force that dick right out the back of my neck!

"Oh, yeah," crooned Clay, "that's done it. That's got him for depth. Now all we have to do is to teach him how to work at that depth, not just gag and moan, like he is now."

"No problem, Mr. B. We'll just move on to these big blue boy-nuts hanging right here."

I felt him grip my ball sack high up and pull the nuts down till they were a tight little circle of taut flesh. My throat was still stuffed with milkmeat but I had stopped the panic-gagging and was trying to do something—anything!—with my tongue and throat muscles that would get the juice flowing so the "experiments" on my own equipment would stop.

"Now, Teddyboy," the Trainer said menacingly, pulling back hard and steadily on my nuts, "we're going to play a little rhythm number on these bongos of yours." Again he started tapping lightly with the crop, only this time on the stretched skin of my balls squeezed down in his fist. "You start squeezing your daddy's dick with your throat muscles, just like swallowing—in time to my beat."

He gave my nuts a sharp rap.

I swallowed, squeezing the meat in my gullet.

Another rap—another swallow.

The pace wasn't too bad, but the blows on my swollen, tender balls were painful.

Then he began to pick up the tempo. The tapping got faster. Before, it had been like "*a-one-and a—two—and a —three—and*

a—four, but now it was more like *onetwothreefour—onetwo-threefour—onetwothreefour*. My throat began to throb in time to the stinging blows.

"Oh, God, Ed," cried Clay, "beat those fuckers. This is great! He's a real rhythm-king on my cock."

Finally, the raps on my nuts were like a crazed drummer riffing in some wild solo. I couldn't keep up. I gasped and grunted and just swallowed and squeezed as fast as I could.

When I thought I would pass out from lack of air and panic and just plain old pain, the drumming stopped. The Trainer said, "That's it for those pretty plumnuts. We don't want to damage him, do we?"

"No, no, of course not," gasped Clay, "but do something else. You've wound him up, let's keep him going. I'm getting ready to feed this kid, if he'll just strip me right."

"I've got just the thing," Ed said quickly. "My own little invention. This will do the trick."

I heard a whirring sound as he grasped my dick firmly and pulled it back through my legs toward him. He pulled it back so far, he must have been looking my cumhole right in the eye.

"I call this my 'peter-eater.' It's named after its big brother, the 'weed-eater.' It's a battery-operated rotary penis whip. These two leather laces whip around in a circle when I press this button. It's got three speeds—Kiss, Bite, and Chew. I just start it rotating, like the cord on a weed-eater, and hold it up to the cockhead, and there he goes!"

I felt a slow flicking against the head of my dick. It was like someone snapping his fingers hard and fast against the sensitive meatus. It was worse than the asshole crop, worse than the drum solo on my nuts—this was hot, stinging snaps on the most sensitive part of my body.

I started to bob up and down on the dick, still deep in my throat. By punishing my tender throat lining with hard cock thrusts, I took away some of the pain in my cockhead—like hitting yourself on the thumb to make you forget the pain in your toe!

Clay liked the up and down lunging motion. "That's it, that's it," he moaned. "Let's go to second speed though, push it up to 'bite.' He needs a little more energy."

The whirring sound changed: it was more like an angry bee or

a wasp now. The whip stings became a constant slashing agony. I bounced my head on Clay's meat—making huge, lunging, swallowing thrusts downward. I reamed out my own throat, rotated my mouth and head to get full pulling and stretching power, jammed my face crazily into his crotch, shaking my skull back and forth, frantic to get the milk to shoot and the whip to stop.

"Now this little sucker's getting to it," Clay yelled. "Now he's doing his job right. Milk that thing! Jerk it around! Oh, yes, Teddy, you're getting there!"

"Shall I go to speed three?" the Trainer asked, cruelly.

"*No, no!*" I tried to beg, as I sucked.

"Go to speed ten, if you want to," Clay shouted wildly, "just make him eat me harder."

There was a blessed break in the dick torture as the Trainer pulled the Peter Eater off my dickhead.

"Got to switch from the leather whips to the denim ones," he explained. "Don't want to mark that juicy cockplum up too badly."

He pressed the third speed button. Now the device gave a high whine. He squeezed my dick even harder and pulled it back tightly between my legs. For a moment he ran his rough thumb over the little lips on my cumhole, probing into the opening, spreading my precum all around it. Then he squeezed the cocktip between steel thumb and forefinger so I felt my cocklips pouch out.

The whine became a white fire, right on my cockslit as the whirling strips began to flick the tip. I lost whatever control I had left. I began to mangle the dick in my mouth. I chewed it, grabbed the shaft in my teeth, jacked it up to the tip with them, mauled the big head with my lips, licked, slobbered, and gnawed all over the balls and back onto the shaft.

"That's got it!" Clay yelled. "Now he's stripping me good. Oh, Teddy, eat your daddy's meat. Keep whipping his cocktip, Ed, make him swallow me whole."

He began to pant and then to take huge, gasping breaths. He grabbed my head and jammed it down on his cock. I was out of my mind with pain and desire. I wanted to feel cum in my mouth more than anything I'd ever wanted in the world. The head of my cock was now burning, and only a load of creamy milk could put out that fire.

Clay began to shudder uncontrollably. His dick swelled up so big I couldn't even move on it. I just rode it, still digging my teeth into the iron-hard shaft and pulling back as hard as I could, shaking my head from side to side like a dog with a rat in its jaws. Suddenly the milk burst out of my daddy's big dickhead into my throat; blasts of creamy liquid shot down my gullet. I pulled up to get some of that soothing liquor in my sore, chafed mouth.

When the Trainer saw the overflow streams of cum washing down Clay's dick shaft, he pulled the Peter Eater away from my cockslit. My concentration lesson was over. Now I could savor the reward, the milky treat which continued to surge in ropes and gobs from daddy's cumhole. He continued to shake and quiver and his words became intelligible again.

"Oh baby, stay on that teat. Keep sucking out that good stuff. Keep your tongue moving around. Eat it all, baby. Drink your milk, suckboy. Drink it all down."

Finally the flow stopped. Clay just lay there, exhausted from his magnificent explosion, the third immense load this evening that I had drawn from that fat, curved milk spout. I still knelt at his teat, with the big, loose milkbags laying spent on the bed below. I rubbed my face slowly all over that crotch, satisfied to have a bellyful of jism and happy to have the Trainer no longer playing his games in my own crotch.

excerpt from
THE MILK FARM
MEMBERS' HANDBOOK

The Staff Compound

The mancows and the staff have their own pool, tennis court, basketball court and gym. These are located in the fenced compound beyond The Milking Barn, where the cow stables, the staff apartments, and the guard barracks are. Clients may observe the staff at play from special viewing points around the edges of the staff compound. A client may request that a staff member or stock cow be brought to him directly from a physical exercise so that he can tongue-wash the sweat-slick body. There is a special fee for this service.

Clients are encouraged to engage Staff in conversation and to mingle with them at the Hotel and on The Milk Farm grounds, BUT NO CLIENT MAY ENTER THE STAFF COMPOUND. ANY CLIENT FOUND IN THE STAFF COMPOUND WILL BE HOOKED UP TO A MECHANICAL MILKING MACHINE FOR 24 HOURS AND THEN BANISHED FROM THE FARM PERMANENTLY.

Clients who attempt to communicate privately with cows or staff for the purpose of enticing them away from The Farm or from the employment of the Pleasure Corporation into personal service or personal relationships will be transported to The Last Resort as permanent Class 4 Slaves.

CHAPTER EIGHT

Test Results

"Well, Sir," the Trainer said, "I think we did it. This little suck-baby finally went the whole hog. All it took was some attention to those sweet cocklips and that tender cumhole with my Peter Eater, and he lost all his inhibitions. It was a real pleasure to watch him give you a thorough milking."

"You're a great teacher, Ed," complimented Clay. "I don't think Teddy had any idea what his mouth was capable of until you gave him the right motivation. I'd like to buy one of those Peter Eaters from you. It would come in very handy."

"I'm sorry, Sir. The Milk Farm owns the patent, since I invented it while working here, and, as you may know, The Milk Farm is very protective of its special equipment. But anytime you've got a boy like Teddy here who needs some concentration lessons, just pay us a visit. I'm always on call."

I was glad to hear that the Peter Eater wasn't going to be part of the home equipment at our house! I was still nursing lazily at Clay's soft meat as he rolled my head around on it, grasping my hair in one hand, squeezing the base of his shaft with the other. The Trainer began to pack up his toys.

"Have you got another client to go to tonight, Ed?" asked Clay.

"No, Mr. B., this is my last job tonight. Why? Did you have something in mind?"

"Call me Clay, and I wasn't thinking about myself—three loads in one evening is my limit. But Teddy here still has his mouth open and his tongue working. I wondered if you'd like to use him. He may be a little tired, but I'm sure there's still some good sucking in him." He pulled my nursing mouth up off his dick. "That right, Teddy?"

"Uh, yes, Sir, I guess so," I mumbled, not sure I could even get my mouth open wide enough to take another hard dick that night.

"That's very generous of you, Clay," Ed answered enthusiastically, "I don't mind if I do pork the kid's mouth before I go. He's

got me damn hot with his fresh asshole and his big boyballs. I'll just take the bar off his knees so he can get down on the floor."

"Why don't you do him here on the bed, so I can watch up close?" suggested Clay.

"Great," Ed agreed. "Lie down on your back, slobberboy. I'm not going to make you suck me. I'm going to fuck your face for you. I'll do all the work this time. You just lay there and keep those slutlips wide open."

I laid down with my head on a pillow right by Clay's side, so he could look down at the action, as Ed crawled onto me, a knee at either side of my face. Then he pulled a long, thin, cut prick out of his black jockstrap. He jacked it slowly as he moved it toward my slack mouth. It hardened into a straight, arrowheaded torpedo, long and lethal looking. He took my head in his hands, interlocking his fingers behind and pulling my face toward his meat. I was caught in the close Vee of his thighs, my neck sharply bent forward for the face fuck. He plugged my throat in one smooth movement, then began long moves in and out, taking his time and working his hips around in a circle so that I felt that narrow cockhead coring out my channel. He liked to keep his meatus in constant contact with the lining of my throat. Sometimes he'd seem to find an especially smooth spot in my gullet, and he'd rub his pointed cockhead across it over and over again, making a purring sound in his own throat as he pleasured himself in mine.

My hands went to my dick, which started to throb in a good way. But they were slapped away by Clay, who pinched my still sore cocklips once, really hard, to remind me that I wasn't allowed to cum. I grunted and involuntarily tightened my throat muscles in reaction to the pain.

"Do that again," ordered Ed, "that was nice."

For the next few minutes my cocklips got squeezed and pinched while I grunted and swallowed around Ed's constantly probing cock. Then he began to go slower and slower until his meat moved in my mouth like a slow-motion nightmare. Finally he came to a complete stop, his penis quivering down the length of my throat. A slow drizzle of thin watery milk trickled down my gullet. It wasn't heavy, but it went on for minutes and he seemed to be in an ecstatic trance the whole time. When it stopped, he jerked out of his dream-state, looked down at my cock-connected face, and

watched his flesh torpedo slip from my lips.

He swung off me, and got up. "That was great, Clay. The puppy's got some fine joy spots in that throat. And he drinks real well. I'm not sure he's a natural cocksucker, but he'll do until one comes along. Thanks for letting me use him."

"My pleasure, Ed. I like the way you shoot, very classy," Clay complimented him. "And I know what you mean about his not being a natural. But face it, some boys were just not born to suck."

This sounded bad. Did it mean I hadn't passed the tests? What was my grade on the "torture suck," as I now thought of it? I couldn't see how anybody could have worked that dick any better than I did. And Clay certainly didn't seem to have any complaints when he was screaming with pleasure and shooting wads of juice in my tired mouth.

Ed packed his things, came over, gave my cock and balls one last groping inspection, and left. I looked up at Clay who still lay with his back up against the headboard.

"What did you mean—I'm not a 'natural'? What was my grade on that last test?"

"I'm tired, Teddy. We'll talk about that tomorrow morning. Now I just want to sleep, but just to keep your mind occupied, I want you to stay on my teat all night long." He slid down on the bed, plumped up his pillows and spread his legs wide. "Get down into your spot between my legs, Teddy, and get my meat back in your mouth where it belongs."

Grumbling, I crawled into position once again, only this time I curled up on my side with my head on his sweaty thigh and nuzzled his semi-hard sticky cock into my mouth, ready to suckle him until morning.

"Get all the way down on it. Don't just mouth the head. My dick wants a warm throat all the way to the root tonight." He guided my head in closer to his pubes. "That's it, nose in there." Little rivulets of juice still squeezed out of his cocklips onto the back of my tongue. I swallowed.

"Now, don't start trying to get me hot again," he cautioned, giving my cheek a light slap, "just nurse it, and maybe in a few hours I'll feed you.

So, after drinking three loads of daddymilk and after getting throat-fucked by a torturer who made my cock feel like it was on

fire, I drifted off to sleep, my sperm-sticky cheek pillowed on a warm thigh, a fleshy hose down my throat, my chin resting against the smooth skin of my daddy's ball sack.

In the morning I woke to find a hard, thrusting tube spurting its morning milk into my stomach. Then I had some "orange juice," fresh squeezed, right from the spout.

❖ ❖ ❖

After we showered together, Clay pinching my cocklips hard to keep me from coming while he soaped up my crotch and asscrack, I started to put on my jeans to go down to breakfast. Clay took them out of my hands.

"I thought we'd sit by the pool and get some sun this morning, Teddy. Get your face rested for the afternoon milking session."

"That'd be great," I said, "but I forgot to bring my swimsuit."

"That doesn't matter. Most of the guys go nude at the pool anyway." He stopped talking suddenly, and a calculating look crossed his face. "I've got an idea that will go towards your punishment for doing such a pisspoor job on your milking tests last night."

He picked up the phone and dialed the desk. "Could you have one of the Pool Boys bring up a pair of shorts for my son? He'd better bring two or three sizes for him to try on. Thanks."

"Are you going to tell me what I did so wrong last night?" I asked, boldly. "Why did you say I wasn't a 'natural'?"

"It's not any one thing, Teddy, it's just your whole attitude." He sat on the bed, looking toward me, standing at the foot. "When the Trainer began to work your dickhead hard with his Peter Eater, you started milking me really well—good depth, hard suction—a real pro dick-stripper. But the fact is that a natural cocksucker wouldn't have needed the Peter Eater to get him to that level of cock eating. Sure, you've got a soft mouth, your throat opens up after a little forcing, and your tongue is pretty versatile, but you just don't seem to have the basic need or desire to get that juice out of that dick. You swallow the cum okay, but you don't really *eat* it. And you don't keep squeezing the head to get out the last good drops. A natural cocksucker is always starved for cum, and when he gets some, he wants it all, and then he wants more. A really prime milker will have to be slapped off a dick he's just pulled, because he keeps jerking on it to get another load. You just

don't have that deep craving for cum." He cocked his eyebrow at me and gave a wry grin. "I think you know what I mean."

"I guess I do," I confessed, "but I really do like to milk dicks, Clay. It's just that it's new to me. I don't know how, yet."

"But that's just my point, Teddy. A 'natural' knows how without being taught. The only teaching a born cocksucker needs is how to discipline his sucking so he doesn't wear his studs out. And maybe to learn the finer points of sucking, like throat rippling, and tongue plugging."

It was crazy to be insulted because somebody told you that you weren't a natural born cocksucker, but that was just what I was feeling. I flopped down on my stomach beside him, with a kind of a "huh" sound, and sulked. He pulled my head up off the sheet by my hair and looked into my scowling face.

"Well, I guess I can't keep my little pussyface from pouting, but I might as well get some use out of that fat lower lip stuck out like that," he said, as he got to his knees and knelt in front of me, pulling my face even further back, so that he could rub the soft tip of his cock across the velvety flesh of the inside of my lower lip. He used his meat like a tool to force my lower lip inside out, further and further down my chin, slicking up his swelling glans with the saliva from my mouth. He took his fist out of my hair, and began to play with my lips. He grabbed my upper lip between thumb and forefinger and pulled it out over his cockhead; with his other hand he pulled my lower lip forward and mashed and molded both around the now slimy head of his penis. For some reason this treatment made my spit flow copiously and I began to drivel all over his hands and his prick. He crooked a thumb in the corner of my mouth and pulled, creating a pocket between my teeth and my cheek and he probed into the warm dripping cavity with his dickhead, squeezing it lightly with his fingers against the outer surface of my cheek. He hooked his thumbs over my front upper and lower teeth and forced my jaw open until I thought it would lock into a permanent yawn. Then he thrust his meat up against the roof of my mouth, pressing the top soft upper palate until I gagged up more saliva. He told me to lift my tongue up, so his cocklips could explore the under surface and down into the mushy hole underneath where my tongue muscle came up from my lower jaw. Then he held the quivering head of his prick just at my open mouth

and made me blow spit bubbles which would just caress the tip of his cumhole before exploding with a wet spray on his crown. He was like a kid with a new plaything. My mouth was a suck-toy and his dick was having a lot of fun with it. I thought maybe I was going to get some warm daddy porridge for my breakfast right there on the bed, but he pulled away when there was a light knock on the door.

"Come on in," he called.

The door opened and a blonde surfer-type dressed in a tank top and loose drawstring trunks came in. He had a gym bag in his hand and a smartass grin on his face. The tank top was cut off above his belly button showing a slim tanned torso; the top said Pool Boy on it.

"Hi," he said, "I'm Bingo. Did you order some swim trunks?"

"Bingo?" Clay sounded amused. "That's a good name—any special significance?"

The boy laughed, showing perfect white teeth. He tossed his shaggy beachboy mane of bleached hair back and looked seductively at Clay from beneath the long bangs that fell to his eyebrows. "That's B for 'Bite Me, Daddy.' I for 'I Gotta Get Sucked,' N for 'Nose On In There, Buddy,' G for 'Go Down, You Fucker,' and O for 'Oh, God, I'm Cumming!' Want to play a game?"

Clay chuckled, "I might teach you some Stud Poker a little later, but for now let's get this boy of mine ready for the pool."

Bingo looked me over as I slumped against the pillows on the bed, my mouth still red and puffy from the mauling it had just taken and my cock sticking up straight in the air drooling gunk down the shaft. "I didn't know what style you had in mind, so I brought several kinds to try out. Is that okay, Mister?" He opened up the bag and dumped several swim suits onto the foot of the bed.

"Let's see what you've got." Clay picked up a pair of baggy trunks like those Bingo was wearing.

"Now the good thing about those," suggested Bingo, "is that they've got plenty of room in case your guy here needs some breathing space for his meat. They'll tent out really nice with a pole like he's got beneath them. Give you something to grab onto if you're in the water and just about to go down, if you know what I mean."

"What do you think, Teddy?" Clay looked at me. "Shall we

stretch this canvas over your tentpole?"

"I don't like those kind of shorts," I pouted. "I think they look crummy."

Bingo blushed and gave me a dirty look, since he was wearing "crummy" shorts just like them.

Clay smirked, enjoying the by-play. "What else have you got there, Bingo?"

"Here's a regular pair of Speedos." He held up a pair of black, classic swimmer's trunks. I perked up a little. This was more like it. Black Speedos would give me some support and not make me look like a bonehead jerk.

"I like those," I said as I crawled down to the foot of the bed to take them from Bingo's hands. "I'll try those on."

Bingo stepped back, holding the swimsuit out of my reach. He looked at Clay. "I could help him try them on," he offered teasingly. "I'm a real pro at getting a tight pair of Speedos on and off a guy."

"That's really nice of you, Bingo." Clay played along. "You'd like Bingo to slip those trunks over your buns, wouldn't you, Teddy?"

Before I could answer with a firm "NO," Bingo jumped in with another suggestion. "It's kinda hot in here, don't you think? Why don't we go out on your balcony and try them on there in the cool morning air?"

What the hell was this jerk talking about? Did he think I was going to stand on our balcony bareass naked and let him dress me up like a Ken doll in front of anybody sitting down on the terrace below?

"Great idea!" Clay took my arm, lifted me off the bed, and pulled me out onto the open balcony before I could even get my mouth open. Bingo followed with the swimsuits bunched in his hands and threw them down on a lounge chair near the wrought iron railing of the balcony. Clay led me near to the edge, just beside the lounge, and then moved to sit at a little table at the other end, about fifteen feet away.

"Hey, Clay, what's up?" Voices came from below. I looked down. Ian and Carlo were sitting on the terrace having their morning coffee and reading newspapers. They could see me standing nude with my dick sticking out and my face getting red.

"We're just picking out a swimsuit for Teddy," Clay looked over the edge of the railing toward the two guys below.

"Need any help?" asked Carlo, eyebrows raised in a mock leer.

"Sure," yelled Clay, "come on up." Both guys got up quickly and moved toward the hotel. It looked like I was going to be the only model in a fashion show on the balcony of our own hotel room! And I wasn't even going to get to dress myself!

I turned and started to go back into the bedroom.

"No, Teddy, you stay right there," Clay ordered sharply. "Just consider this as part of your punishment for failing your exams last night."

Bingo looked quizzically at Clay. "Just a little private matter between the two of us," he explained. "For now, why don't you lay out the different suits along the railing, so they'll be ready for trying on when the other guys get here."

I glared at Bingo as he made a big production of stringing the small pieces of cloth along the balcony's edge. He would hold up each one and taunt me with it: some of them didn't look big enough to cover my nose, let alone my dick. Soon Ian and Carlo came into the room and out onto the balcony, joking about the "fashion show" and complimenting me on my "looks."

"We told the front desk to send us up a continental breakfast for four," said Ian. "I hope that's okay with you, Clay. Or maybe you've already eaten." He looked slyly at my dripping prick.

"No, Teddy's ham and eggs haven't been tasted yet. I'm saving that for later in the day," explained Clay.

"I hope our breakfast is served by that cute English Muffin," joked Carlo, "the one with the cockney accent and buttery buns."

"You've got good American buns at home," Ian jibed. "You don't need to go looking for any foreign ones."

Bingo broke into this banter, "Shall I try these Speedos on your boy, Mister?"

"Yeah," Clay answered, "let's dress this doll up."

Bingo moved behind me. He put his lips near my ear and said softly, "Put your hands up behind your head, doll baby, and lift up your right foot a little." He slipped the leg opening of the Speedos over my foot and then over the other. Once the trunks were around my ankles he began to work them slowly up my legs, letting his hands and his arms come into maximum contact with

my calves and the backs of my thighs. My dick got even harder with these sly caresses. Gradually he pulled them up onto my hips so the waist band caught just below my balls. Then he put the palms of his hands on my ass and inched the stretch material over my cheeks, letting my meat and nuts hang out over the front edge which got tighter and tighter against my thighs, pushing my equipment up and forward obscenely.

Clay and the two other men at the table made appropriate dirty comments during all this, and suggestions about other little maneuvers Bingo could do to get me even hotter. Finally he began to pull the front of the trunks up over my cock and balls. This involved a lot of finger work on my meat and repeated tugging and tucking to get the whole massive swollen works under the stretched fabric. When he finished he stood to the side, gave my butt a hard smack and cried, "It's Mr. Speedo, gentlemen, what do you think?"

Clay ordered me over to the table, making me keep my hands clasped behind my neck. The three of them pawed me, pinching my ass, poking their fingers up against the material covering my asshole, moving my dick around into different positions, until my whole crotch was wet with the precum constantly leaking from my meat which ached for release. These games were interrupted by the Room Waiter who rolled a cart full of breakfast goodies out onto the balcony. While they buttered their croissants and poured out their coffee, I was led back to the lounge by Bingo, who took off the Speedos with the same teasing moves he had used to put them on. He worked from behind me and pressed his body up against mine as he slid the trunks back down my legs. His tongue licked into the cleft of my ass as he fumbled the suit off my feet and he probably would have gone in even more deeply if Clay hadn't told him to get on with the show.

After that he tried me in a bikini suit which was even smaller than the Speedo and so tight that my dick lay sideways along my upper thigh filling out the red stretch-pouch clear to my hipbone. Carlo got so excited at this "look" that he took out his own brown cock and began to stroke it. The Room Waiter hadn't left: he stood behind the table enjoying the show with the others, and Carlo motioned him around to his crotch where the waiter crouched and gently licked the shiny purple glans of Carlo's meat.

The bikini was followed by a bright yellow jock strap which hugged my cock and balls closely, forcing my steel rod painfully down in a long throbbing arc. The yellow leg straps were so tight, they pushed my ass cheeks up into pink round balloon bubbles which Clay and Ian slathered with butter and strawberry jam: they licked the sweet mixture off gleefully while Carlo unloaded into the Room Waiter's sucking throat. By this time Bingo's own loose shorts were well-tented and he forced my hand onto his pole, making me handmilk him while my butt got buttered and jammed. When he was about to cum, he pulled down the front of his suit and moved around behind me, where Ian and Clay were still licking their breakfast buns. Moving in close beside them, he took his skinny cock in hand and shot several wads of cumbutter to mix with the real butter on my ass. Then all *five* of them, Clay, Ian, Carlo, the Room Waiter, *and* Bingo got down and pigged out on my jockstrapped, jam-covered buns, licking and biting until I thought I would finally shoot my load. But Clay was too canny to let that happen. He pushed me away from those five hungry mouths before I could cum, and had the Room Waiter clean me up with a towel while they all cooled off.

It looked as if all the suits had been tried, until Bingo said, "I've brought a special item which might just do the trick for you, Sir, if you want to see it." He pulled out of the gym bag a last pair of shorts. They were white and seemed somehow strange. As he held them up, I realized what was wrong with them. They had no crotch room at all. In fact they looked like women's shorts—the kind that zip up the side and fit so tight through the crotch that you can practically see the lips of the cunt beneath. *And that's just what they were!*

"These are actually ladies' shorts," explained Bingo, "but we use them for special occasions when clients want to see everything a staff member's got—and I do mean everything, down to the tiniest bump of a cocklip."

Clay was enthusiastic. "Now I think maybe we're getting somewhere," he said. "Get those suckers on him."

Not only were the women's white shorts not made for any man and his equipment, this particular pair were about three sizes too small for me! Bingo had to inch them up over my thighs and hips, squeezing my flesh bit by bit into their constricting grip. When he

finally got the side zipper closed, I felt as if I was caught in a strong vise around the middle part of my body. But worse was the position of my cock and my nuts. Since there was no place for them to go, they swelled out the front grotesquely, showing off every vein and hair. The white cotton of the shorts was strong, but a little stretchy: Bingo went to the table, picked up a glass of water and brought it back toward me. He casually poured the water down the front of the suit and I realized that the wet cotton became almost transparent, covering my dick and balls like a thin rubber sheet. There were lots of naked guys and lots of cocks and balls hanging out in the open at The Milk Farm, but somehow this spectacle of my own penis and testicles swelling out the wet front of a pair of white shorts was lewder and sexier than anything I'd seen. The other guys seems to feel the same way. They got quiet and stared at the package of meat which bulged in my crotch. The air was heavy with desire. Bingo played up to the atmosphere. He began to run his hands over the contours of my sex.

"There are several ways you can wear this," he crooned. His hands began molding the flesh beneath the wet cotton, like a sculptor molding clay. "Some like to see the cock and balls forced to one side of this strong center seam which runs under the crotch." He pressed my meat across my pubic area until both dick and nuts were caught against my right thigh. "Others will pull the dick straight up along the center seam with the balls puffing out on either side." He worked my hard dick up against my stomach. The head popped out the top of the waistband, and my nuts swelled out like fat squirrel cheeks on either side of the seam below. "The good thing about this arrangement," he said, "is that the cumhole is out in the open, standing up, and ready for licking." With that he leaned down and ran his hot tongue over my slimy cockhead, tickling my cocklips with little stabs of his tongue tip. By now I had my hands behind my back instead of behind my neck, and I started to bring them forward to force that smug face down onto my prick; to gag him with all the cum that was building up inside me. But he was quick, moving behind, grabbing my wrists firmly and bringing my arms back into the braced position again. "And, finally, the position I personally like best, the meat down one leg and the balls down the other." He pushed my penis down toward my thigh, letting the strong center seam of the shorts cut up at the

base separating my two balls onto the other side. My dick was so much longer than the shorts that once again the crown popped out and showed beneath the edge of the right leg opening. My meat twisted to accommodate the pressure and the seam so that the underside of my prick now faced outward, and the sensitive triangular frenulum skin was open to all comers. Bingo put his thumb against that soft triangle of flesh and pressed, causing even more precum to flow out my cumhole and down onto my thigh, where it glistened like the trail of a slug crawling across a stone. "For a leaker, like your boy here, this 'split' position is ideal. You can just put your finger down against his thigh and scoop up the honey." And he did just that, lifting his honey covered fingertip to his red lips which sucked noisily at it.

Clay sprang out of his chair, grabbed Bingo's arm, pulled him into the room, threw him face up on the bed and sank his raging cock deep into the astonished boy's mouth. Within seconds Bingo was gurgling and choking around a hot wash of Clay's sperm, while Ian and Carlo just sat on the balcony still staring at me. Suddenly I realized that we had other observers as well. Down below, on the terrace, several club members and staff stood gaping up at me, open mouthed, with greedy eyes. The Room Waiter came up to me and murmured into my ear, "Baby, if you go down to the pool in those shorts, you're going to be the most popular girl at the ball. Your dance card is going to be filled twenty times over."

*   *   *

As it turned out, the white shorts were just too tight. I could barely move in them, and there was no question of being able to kneel down for my milking sessions. Sitting would have de-nutted me for life, I think. So I ended up in the Speedos, which, after the ladies' shorts, the jockstrap, and the bikini, felt like a comfortable pair of baggy trousers.

I still hadn't had any breakfast, so after Bingo took away his swimsuit collection and after Ian and Carlo went along to their room to take the edge off the horniness the fashion show had given them, Clay had the Room Waiter bring me a solid meal of waffles and sausage (the real kind, not the man-kind). He put on his swimming trunks while I was eating and then we went down for some sun around the pool.

excerpt from
THE MILK FARM
MEMBERS' HANDBOOK

The Milk Farm Neck and Wrist Strap Code

Members will note that staff personnel (excluding mancow stock) sometimes wear neck and wrist straps in different colors. The significance of these is given below. All services arising from the use of strapped personnel are subject to special fees.

Any staff members wearing a RED NECK STRAP will give cocksuck service to climax immediately on request anywhere and at any time. Staff with BLACK NECK STRAPS may be reserved for special cocksuck service through the front desk at a time and place to be arranged.

Any staff member wearing RED WRIST STRAPS can be milked until he cums at any time and anywhere upon the client's order. Staff members wearing BLACK WRIST STRAPS can be milked by arrangement with the front desk, where a time and place for the milking will be scheduled. The wrist straps can be attached behind the back by a six-inch chain which each staff member carries if the client prefers to have him restrained for pulling.

Members of Maintenance Staff and Grounds Personnel may be found wearing BROWN WRIST STRAPS. This indicates that the staff member will face-fuck the client upon request wherever he happens to be working. Clients using BROWN WRIST-STRAPPED personnel should expect verbal abuse and rough deep throat plugging from an aggressive man who will remain fully clothed.

CHAPTER NINE

Teddy Gets His Reward

As we came down the stairs toward the Hotel lobby, a man stepped out of an office next to the reception desk. Clay introduced him as Jack Devlin, the Manager of The Farm. He was a tall, slightly menacing man. The black pupils of his piercing hazel eyes watched like a lizard or a snake. His face was drawn and weathered, with a sharp, handsome nose and firm no-nonsense lips. He looked as if he had been through a lot and seen everything.

"That was quite a show you gave us on the balcony this morning, Clay," he said with an unreadable expression on his face. Clay seemed nervous.

"I hope you weren't offended, Jack. We didn't realize we had such an audience."

"No, no, I enjoyed the spectacle. Your boy here has star potential, I think." He looked me up and down, his gaze coming briefly to rest on the lump in my Speedos. "In fact I've had several enquiries from clients wondering if he was a staff boy or not. I was thinking that maybe we could make him an honorary employee of The Farm for the day, maybe let him wear a red strap on his neck, give that mouth a little more practice." He put a leathery brown hand to my face and rubbed his thumb over my lips. I felt my cock shiver at his touch.

"Great idea, Jack," agreed Clay. "I know he'd like that, wouldn't you, Teddy?" He looked at me intently, seeming to *will* me to answer "yes," which must have worked, because that's exactly what I did.

The Manager brought out one of the red leather bands I'd seen on many of the employees around The Farm and buckled it around my neck. "I'm sure you've realized by now," he said, standing back to look at me with my new decoration, "that our straps provide certain messages to our clients. This red neck band, for example, tells any of our customers that its wearer is available for immediate suck service wherever he's commanded. You won't have any trou-

ble with that, will you, boy?"

"He'll be fine, Jack," Clay broke in nervously. "He'll get down on his knees and take anything that's put in his face. I'll see to that."

Jack Devlin stared at Clay for a moment with what seemed to me to be a kind of contempt. "We'll credit any suck-charges he earns against your bill." He turned and abruptly walked back into his office.

We went out onto the terrace and found Ian and Carlo sunning by the pool. Wesley sat on the edge of a lounge chair beside them, fully dressed. "Well, well," he exclaimed, "a new temptation in this Garden of Eden. Have you sold this dear boy into slavery, Clay?"

Clay ignored the question. "Why are you dressed up for a tea party, Wesley?" he teased.

"I'm just waiting for the limousine from The Fuck Corral. I go over every morning during my stays here for a little light stuffing," he said, archly.

Ian piped up, "He says that getting his asshole reamed out by one of the Corral's Pro Fuckers makes him a better cocksucker."

"I doubt if I've ever used quite those coarse terms, but substantially what Ian says is true," huffed Wesley.

"I wouldn't mind doing a little stuffing myself this morning," Clay admitted. "The Milk Farm's a great place, but their ban on ass-fucking the staff is a drag."

"Well, come along with me, Clay," Wesley urged. "You know that the Corral serves up some prime asspussy as well. Bring the boy, make it a party."

"No, Teddy's got to stay here. I'm saving his ass for another visit. He's got too many other lessons to learn just now."

"Leave him here, then," Wesley suggested. "He's a big boy, he can take care of himself, and with that red necklace he'll be taking care of plenty of others this morning as well."

"The problem is that I really need someone to babysit him— or cocksit him I might say," Clay reached down and squeezed my bulge in his hand. "This teat is being saved for a special surprise this afternoon, so somebody's got to see that he doesn't shoot before I get back."

I felt like a naughty kid whose parents couldn't find him a sit-

ter. I looked down at Carlo, who had been ogling me with great interest during this chat.

"Don't look at me, kid," he said. "Ian and I have a tennis court booked in ten minutes. The winner of our match gets to be King for a Night, and I've got some great ideas to make this pansy of mine squirm after I beat the jock off him today."

"Yeah, sure," Ian challenged, "the last time you won, the most interesting thing you could think of was to make me eat a weenie out of your butt. Very original."

Wesley stood and took Clay by the arm. "Listen, I've got the perfect solution. You see that big blonde thing over there? The one The Farm calls the Lifeguard for this kiddie pool? Well, he's got nothing better to do all day than sit in that tall chair and pretend he doesn't know how pretty he is. Ask him to keep an eye on Teddy."

Clay walked over to the Lifeguard's chair and talked with the guy sitting there. They looked back toward me several times, and finally the guard motioned me over.

"Teddy, this is Sean. He's going to take care of you while I'm gone for a couple of hours. Do what he says, and don't let anybody work your meat." Then he left me in the tender care of Sean the Blonde Beast.

He looked more like the halfback on an Ivy League football team than a lifeguard—a clean-cut preppy jock, with short brown hair in a brush cut. Not beefy, but getting there. Dangerous green eyes peered steadily at me from beneath slightly up-slanted brows. He had a straight nose, wide, spreading to sensuous nostrils, and a thin, but well-shaped upper lip, slightly smiling, above a full, fleshy lower lip thrust out in the pout of a permanent surliness. It was a face which seemed to say "You want this? Just try to come and get it!" His body was going to be massive eventually, but he looked young, maybe a couple of years older than me, and it wasn't quite ripe yet: thick neck on wide shoulders, pecs still in the forming stage, their lower curves soft and sketchy, the abs just barely defined beneath an all-over glow of tan. I could have fallen for the guy like a girl falls for the Homecoming King, but there wasn't time. Sean the Beast wasn't looking for romance.

"Climb up on the ladder rung of my chair and get your slut-mouth in my crotch," he ordered, not lovingly at all. I climbed up

on the six inch step that brought my head level with the spread
of his thighs. He was nude, although apparently The Farm management expected him to wear the standard red swim trunks of
a lifeguard, because a pair hung on the chair arm beside him. His
cock was just fist-long, but with a broad helmet-head larger than
the shaft behind it, making the whole thing look blunt and aggressive. The flesh of the meaty crown was shiny and wet, with rosy
highlights on its curves. He had firm balls well-packed into their
slightly stretched sack. I was experienced enough by now to know
that the cock looked suckable. I could probably swallow the length
down to his pubes without forcing, but then what about the
width? That might take some doing. And I knew that I could never
get both those balls into my mouth at the same time. But his attitude seemed to say that *he* would get them in there, no matter
what I felt about it.

"What're you waiting for, kid? Get down on it." He spread his
beefy thighs wider and I leaned in to take him. It wasn't long before I realized that I didn't seem to be making him very happy, with
my little licks and dabs—the repertory of suck techniques I had
learned the night before during my "tests." "What is this shit?" he
growled. "That red strap on your neck says that you can SUCK!
So DO IT!"

I worked at the threatening thickness of his meat for a few more
minutes, until he grabbed my hair in a fist and pulled my face
rudely off it. "I can see this calls for some suck discipline, boy. I'm
going to have to tie you down to your duty."

He took off the whistle he had around his neck and threaded
the double cord through two metal loops on the front of my neck
strap. Then he pulled my mouth brutally onto his cock, pressing
against my head until his fat mushroom crown jammed the back
of my throat. If I was careful, and didn't panic, I could just breathe
through my nose, so long as he didn't try to force the rod any
deeper. Then he took the cord attached to the loops on my neck
band and pulled the two ends up tight so that I couldn't have
backed off his cock even if I'd wanted to. He wrapped the ends
of the cord several times around the base of his cock and balls, and
tied it off. My mouth was effectively and actually fixed to his
crotch: he wore my head like the big pouch of a jockstrap.

"There you go, cockbaby," he announced in a cruelly satisfied

voice. "I've given you your bottle, now suck on it."

For what seemed like a lifetime I struggled with the tube in my throat, swallowing over and over again to keep from gagging and choking myself on a bone that couldn't be spit out. These swallowing movements seemed to please him, because his penis started flexing and throbbing in time to them. One of The Farm's clients came up to the chair and asked him if he could use my mouth when Sean was through with it.

"Fuck off, creep," was Sean's gracious reply. "I haven't even started with this puppy yet."

Sometime after that, his organ began to flutter uncontrollably on my tongue and I felt his balls pull up tight against my chin, signalling the flood that was to come. I didn't get to taste any of the hot eruption: the head was too far back in my throat, but I felt splatters of semen against the sore lining, coating it with a soothing warmth.

He left me tied to his dick for a long time after that as he squeezed my head between his thighs and rolled it lazily around the softening shaft with his hands.

Then, almost before I knew what was happening, I found myself on my hands and knees in the pool house with Sean the Beast preparing to fuck the virgin ass that Clay had said was to be saved for some later time.

A pool boy had come to give Sean his half-hour break, and the lifeguard had taken me with him, although he had the courtesy to untie my head from his crotch and let me walk at his side toward the small room which he used as his own private dressing area and lounge. Once inside he stripped off my suit, and bounced my aching, cum-filled balls up and down on his hand. But it wasn't my crotch that interested him. Soon he had me lie down on the floor and he straddled my head from the top, looking toward my cock and nuts. He leaned down and locked his arms under my thighs, pulling my legs and lower torso up and over so that I was curled into a bodyball with my neck against the concrete floor and my asshole open right before him. He sank down on his haunches so that his nuts and dick hung into my mouth and ordered me to lick them while he played with my ass.

He pushed his thumbs down into my hole and pressed the ring open, spitting down into it, to make the whole area slick for his

probing fingers. He ran his forefinger around the edge of the opening, pressing to show more of the pink inside. He leaned down and
licked me, fucking his muscular tongue down into the lining of my
channel. I had never felt such thrilling waves of pure pleasure before in my life. I wanted it to go on forever.

But then he rolled me over roughly, jerked me to my knees,
pressed hard on my back so my head went to the floor, my face
crushed against the cold cement, and knelt behind me so that I
could feel the steel bar of his dick nudge into the cleft of my ass.
"Time to pork this honeybutt," he said with an urgent huskiness.
"Time to make you squeal, little piggy."

He leaned forward on my back and brought the squared-off
fingertips of one hand to my mouth, forcing them in, ordering me
to slick them up with my spit. He pushed four fingers so deeply
into my throat that I gagged and coughed up streams of saliva,
which he carried back to his cock and my asshole, coating them
with the mouth lube. Then he began to use the plump head of his
fuckpole to circle the pucker of my hole, teasing it with little jabs,
drawing away and pinching the tender flesh between his fingers,
then pressing again with his knob in a slow tormenting spiral until
at last I felt the tight ring of my sphincter close over the deep flange
of his glans. There was sharp pain, but the promise of pleasure
also, and I instinctively began to press back against the invader.
But Sean the Beast wasn't ready for such an easy conquest. He held
my hips firmly and kept me from surrounding the shaft of his cock
with my asscunt. He circled his own hips, keeping the head of his
dick right at my tight ring, reaming it out, stretching it in the corkscrew motion of his tool.

But it turned out that I wasn't to get fucked by Sean the Beast
after all.

"TEDDY, ARE YOU IN THERE?" Carlo's voice broke the
flow of rising passions. There was a pounding on the locked door.
"Sean, open up, NOW!" Jack Devlin's voice was added to the bab-
ble, and then there was the sound of a key fumbling in the lock.
Sean had frozen at the sound of the Manager's voice. As the door
crashed open, he pulled out of my ass in a panic and scrambled
across the floor toward the far wall, his face a mask of frustrated
lust and fright.

Carlo and Ian picked me up and hustled me out of the room.

I caught a glimpse of Jack Devlin advancing slowly toward the cowering Lifeguard before the door slammed shut.

So my ass was still (mostly) virgin, although I had gotten an exciting glimpse of pleasures I had never dreamed of.

My two "saviors" took me up to their room, quizzing me about my "rape." Ian stuck his hand down the front of my swimming suit and groped my stocky cock to make sure that I hadn't shot. Then he went in to shower off the sweat of the tennis match, which he had won, leaving me with his lover. Carlo decided that he might as well get a tongue bath while he was waiting for his turn in the shower and I got my first taste of the ripe juice that a man collects in his armpits and in the crack of his butt when he plays in the hot sun. As I was licking the moist triangle between his thighs just below his balls, he began to moan and squirm until finally he pulled my face up to his short, thick cock and added his cum to the mingled flavors of his sweat and funk.

While Carlo was in the shower, Ian let me tongue the lotion of my saliva onto his nipples and down his stomach, rewarding me with a fragrant cream of his own from a long, elegant prick.

When Clay returned, looking mellow and loose after his fuck, he found me with a well-used mouth, and a still unsucked cock desperate to cum.

At lunch, which I spent beneath the table of four clients who requested the pleasure of my company and fed me slabs of meatloaf and hot potatoes, Jack Devlin came into the dining room and made an announcement.

"Gentlemen, this will be Punishment Day in The Milking Barn. In addition to our usual milking stock, we will have two stalls devoted to some of our Staff fuckups who need a little rough pulling."

This was greeted with applause and whistles of approval around the room.

"In addition," Devlin continued, "there will be a special event of the sort that all of you dream about. That's all I'll say now about that, but we'll expect to see you there at three o'clock sharp. The milking begins one hour later than usual, because today we're going to keep the Barn open continuously until midnight. A buffet will be served at the refreshment bar there and you can eat and drink at your leisure. So rest up for an hour or so, and get those

mouths ready for a real feast."

From my spot underneath a table, crouched between the thighs of a university professor from New Orleans, I wondered if I'd have an appetite for milkteats that afternoon, after the cream I'd swallowed since the fashion show on the balcony that had started my day.

Back in the room Clay suggested we take a snooze, and we laid on the bed beside each other without even touching until I drifted off into a fitful dream of lifeguard whistles and concrete floors.

The phone woke us and Clay muttered, "Hell, we're late," after he'd listened to whoever had called. He made me take a quick shower and then hurried me to The Milking Barn. I wasn't in a good mood. I couldn't see the point in rushing to pull some more teats with a mouth that was tired from its morning attentions to all comers, and my blueballs were killing me with the frustration of denied release for the last day and a half—two days, really, since I hadn't jerked off since the Thursday before we came to The Farm.

When we entered the big room with the long rows of stalls down each side, the center aisle was full of men all looking toward us expectantly. Toward the far end Jack Devlin was standing on a platform with a pin-spotlight shining down on him. He looked pissed-off, as if he'd been waiting hours for a guest to arrive at a party. But as we approached through the crowd, his expression became more friendly and he started his speech.

"Gentlemen, this is one of our special surprise milking events—a 'Punishment Pull.' We've brought in seven staff members—not regular studcow stock—who've fucked up in their duties so badly that they need the discipline of a few hours in the stalls. We've got a couple of Room Boys who didn't give the members complete satisfaction; we've got Frank, the front desk clerk at the Hotel, who screwed up the list of charges on a member's bill; there is a Nutboy who couldn't take what was dished out to him during a munch-and-crunch session in a member's room; there's a Lab Assistant who left a milking-machine on too long and put a prize cow's teat out of commission for a couple of days; and there's a gardener who got a little too enthusiastic in a member's mouth. That's six fuckups who will be strapped into Stalls H and I and who can be rough-pulled or ball-milked until the Milk Master says

they've had all they can take (and maybe a little more!)."

This news was greeted with fervent applause and shouts of approval, but one voice called out, "Who's the seventh fuckup today?"

"I know that many of you will be very happy to hear," answered the Manager, "that our very naughty boy with the bad attitude, Lifeguard Sean, will be strapped down in the Private Box Stall to be punished at your pleasure."

The joy that this announcement created was a sign of how many customers, besides me, Sean the Beast had offended. As he was led forward, his red neck band attached to a lead-rope in the hands of one of the Milking Assistants, several guys began to call for first crack at him in the closed half-box next to the stall where I had drunk my first man-milkshake the previous afternoon. But it was the Major who got the nod from Jack Devlin and the look on the Blonde Beast's face when he realized that he was going to be shut up in a closed space with the Terror of The Milk Farm seemed to satisfy some of the clients as much as an actual session with him would have.

But before the crowd could break up to go its way to the regular milking stalls or to the special punishment stations, the Manager held up his hand for quiet and added one last item to his list of special pleasures.

"I know you've all enjoyed watching the antics of one of our new customers this weekend as he's learned the ways of The Milk Farm. Some of you have even helped to break him in by giving him something to focus his oral attentions on. I'm talking, of course, about Teddy here, Clay Brock's boy."

All eyes now turned to me, and Clay pushed me closer to the platform where Jack was standing. The Manager put his hand on my shoulder and continued.

"This weekend visit to The Farm is Teddy's graduation treat and we don't want him to go away without a special gift from the Management and the membership. So, this afternoon this handsome, horny, unpulled hunk of baby beef is going to get milked, and he's going to get milked good!"

At first there was just an intense silence as all eyes sharpened and stared even more greedily at me. Then a cheer broke out and wild applause and whistling followed. Jack Devlin had to shout

over the noise:

"AND TO START THE FESTIVITIES"—the crowd quieted down—"to start the festivities we're going to put Teddy on the spinner and give him a Merry-Go-Round Pull so you can all get a splash of his first shoot."

He stepped off the platform and I now saw that it was a small round wheel and that out of its center there rose a six-foot pole with ropes and straps hanging at intervals down its length. I was lifted up to stand on the wheel, and as my body was fastened to the pole, with my hands bound and behind my neck, and ankles strapped firmly to prevent more than minimal movement, I realized that the wheel and the stake were on ball-bearings and that the whole apparatus could turn, like a playground merry-go-round.

"As some of you know," explained Jack, "a Merry-Go-Round Pull is not a mouth pull, it's a handjob. The Milk Master will apply his skilled fist to this young stud's cock and bring him to the shooting point, and if you'll all move up close and surround the wheel, sitting or kneeling on the floor around it, you'll get the first hot spray from his teat in your faces."

And that's how it went—my first orgasm at The Milk Farm. The Milk Master would tug at my swollen cock for a few moments, then give the wheel a hard push, putting me into a fast spin with my prick whipping in the air. Then he'd stop the motion and give me a few more strokes, followed by another dizzying rotation. The centrifugal force of each spin seemed to draw my cum up farther and more urgently into my cock, until finally, after an especially fast whirl, his insistent squeezing of my milkmeat brought me to the edge and I began to cum. Just at the moment of climax he gave the wheel the hardest push of all and my pulsing cock spurted a hot, swirling rain of semen over the hungry faces held up to bathe in it. As the circling wheel came slowly to a stop, there was a long moment filled only with the sounds of cum being scraped from foreheads and cheeks and slurped off fingers into wet mouths. I had fed the multitude with my manna!

After that, things got more down-to-earth. I was taken to a regular station in the Pure Whole Milk Stall where I had first pulled Rusty, and strapped to the wall with two regular stock cows. My first mouth-pull was Ian, who turned out to be a voracious, ath-

letic milker. He attacked my teat with unrelenting vehemence and suctioned my second load of juice with shattering teeth-jerks on my shaft and sharp tongue-jabs down into my spasming cumslit. Then, unlike regular stock who got a rest after each pull, the Milk Master allowed me to be pulled once again, this time by Carlo who surprisingly babied my dick with a soft, caressing suckle and gently rolled my balls in his fingers, teasing out my third load, which was a mellow drizzle of thin fluid. He patted my flank as he rose, and said in my ear, "I'll bet you thought Ian would be the soft-milker in this family, didn't you? Never misjudge an intellectual—they can be mean suckers!"

Now the Milk Master had me taken back to the stock lounge for a rest. Clay was nowhere in sight. In fact I couldn't remember seeing him since I caught a glimpse of his face flashing by during that last orgasmic spin. As we walked down the back passageway that ran behind the line of milking stalls, I heard muffled groans coming from behind one of the doors.

"That's Lifeguard Sean getting his punishment," explained the Milking Assistant. "Would you like to take a look?"

I said I would like to see what was happening to Sean the Beast if it was allowed, and the Assistant opened the door leading into the back of the closed stall. There I saw a tableau unlike anything in my experience.

Sean lay on a padded narrow table; his legs were spread wide and his ankles were cuffed; the cuffs were attached to ropes which ran up into pulleys on the ceiling and they had been stretched up and back so that his ass rested just at the end of the table. Milking Assistants stood on either side, and Sean's fists were wrapped around their hard dicks, milking them in a frenzied jerking rhythm. This frenzy was the result of something which sent shivers down my spine.

The Major stood at the end of the table, facing into those widespread legs, his fist buried almost up to his elbow in the Lifeguard's asshole. I could see grease bubbling up out of the hole around the rubber-gloved arm which the Major slowly corkscrewed in and out of the stretched opening. With his other hand the Major held Sean's thick penis so tight that his swollen cockhead pulsed purple above the edge of his fist. But the scene wasn't complete yet.

I saw that each of the Assistants had an implement in their

hands. One held a long pliable rod with a small black square on its end, like a tiny fly-swatter. He was rubbing this square over the pouting cocklips of Sean's meatus, and from the cries and groans coming from Sean's gagged mouth it was clear that the surface of the square was rough and grainy, like sandpaper. After a minute or so of this, the Major would shout "STINGER" and the other Assistant would bring his implement into play. This was another flexible rod—plastic maybe—with no special tip. At the command, the sandpaper tool was quickly moved away, and the other Assistant flicked the wicked looking rod sharply, right on the victim's cumhole. This created a tremendous heaving and jerking in Sean's muscular body, and his hands jacked the Assistants' dicks madly while the Major kept up his relentless twisting up the spasming ass.

Finally the jerking had its desired effect and the two Assistants simultaneously pushed away Sean's hands and held their gushing pricks on the purple head of the dick the Major continued to squeeze. That was a cue for the Major to lunge down and roughly lick the juice off the swollen glans. This licking in turn brought Sean to climax; with a muffled roar, his body arched and strained upward. The Major released his hold on the dickshaft and gobbled voraciously at the spurting cream, still working his fist in the hole beneath. And he didn't stop as the flow dribbled to its end. Pulling his lips back from his wolfish teeth he gnawed and chewed at the cockhole until the Lifeguard's cries became nothing more than a continuous high-pitched keening.

I was so shaken by what I had witnessed that I barely realized the Assistant had pulled me back into the hallway, and was guiding me again toward the stock lounge. I felt sorry for poor Sean the Blonde Beast. Even though he had abused me, I thought the punishment was way out of proportion to the crime!

The lounge was a big room filled with comfortable chairs and sofas, along with a few daybeds where spent studcows were recuperating from pulls. The guys looked at me curiously, knowing that I wasn't really one of them, then turned back to their conversations. I sat and listened in a half-awake daze, getting my strength back after three tumultuous shoots.

"So now The Master says I've got to let the bastard go on to a 5-6-7 pull this evening," a small tough looking punk was saying.

"The creep has gummed my teat four times since two o'clock and every time I've had a harder job feeding him. I can probably do the fifth shoot okay if Master lets my joy button get zapped while the guy works me, and maybe load number six can be talked out—the Lab geeks have put some kind of post-hypnotic spell on me and they say that the right words will trigger a shoot—but, Jesus, I don't know where the fuck the milk for number seven is going to come from."

Another of the men sitting nearby spoke up. "Did I ever tell you about the time I fed this milker one big fat pearl of cum on my seventh shoot? It just oozed out, about the size of a white jelly-bean, and plopped down on his tongue. That stuff was so potent, I heard the guy actually staggered like he was drunk when he walked back to the Hotel. He told Mr. Devlin that he used to wake up in the middle of the night for months afterwards with the taste of my cum-pearl in his mouth."

I felt the touch of a hand on my arm and opened my eyes to look into the face of an angel. He seemed to be about the same age as me, but he was thinner and had a classic beauty—the look of a young poet with sculpted lips, a straight aristocratic nose, dark lashes fringing haunted eyes, his hair a tangle of blonde curls. He was squatting down by the big easy chair I was sitting in.

"I'm Tim," he said, "but they call me Honeyboy here. What's your name."

"Teddy—I'm just called Teddy," I replied, almost tongue-tied in the presence of such beauty. He stood up to move around to the empty chair beside me, and it was then that I saw his slender, lightly muscled torso, a long expanse of flesh down to a blonde bushy pubis where my image of an angelic, aristocratic young poet got knocked for a loop. Between his narrow, streamlined thighs hung a solid, heavily-veined, broad-headed club, as long and as massive as a horse-penis. And behind, there was a bulging sack of ball meat, the nuts hanging as low as the head of his cock. The contrast between the sensitive boyish face and body and the monstrous mancock and bull balls was so astonishing I couldn't look away.

"Yeah, I know," he said shyly, "it's freakish. It's what my uncle's had them do to me here. When I was brought to The Farm about a year ago, I had a dick about the size of yours. Then they started

pumping me like crazy. At first I thought it was cool; it made me feel tough and really manly, walking around with a big meatbat swinging between my legs, but then they just kept pumping, every day for hours at a time, till now I have this humongous 'thing' in my crotch. And it leaks all the time—that's why they call me Honeyboy. You want to touch it? Go ahead, all the guys play with it. I like to have it stroked."

I reached forward across the arm of his chair, putting my hand on the python of penis flesh which lay on the cushion of balls between his wide-spread legs. It felt warm and spongy and made you want to take it in both hands and squeeze.

"What're you here for?" he asked, cocking one leg over the arm of the chair so I could get at him better. "You going to come into the system?"

"No, no," I said confidently, "I'm only here on a visit because I just got out of high school and my stepdad thought this would be a good present. Getting milked in the Barn was kind of a surprise gift from Mr. Devlin." I was pulling his meat with both hands now: a stream of amber syrup flowed from the thick-lipped cum-slit.

"Take a drink, if you want to," he offered. "One old guy who rents me by the hour in the 'Honeysuckle Room' over at the Hotel says it tastes like fifty-year-old cognac."

I almost had my tongue at the oozing hole, when one of the Milking Assistants slapped my head away and said, "Lay off Honeyboy's sauce, kid. That's for the paying customers only."

"I'm a paying customer," I objected.

"Not today, you're not," he replied, leering. "Today you're just one of the cowboys and it's time for you to go out and feed the customers again." He pulled me up and began to walk me toward the door. I looked back at Tim. He watched me go with longing eyes.

In the stalls once more, I began to lose track of all the mouths that pulled at my flagging cock. Some I fed, others just hauled and yanked on my flesh until the Milk Master warned them off. But still he didn't release me. He only warned my milkers that I was "dry" and that the best they could expect was a dribble of the last of my nectar. But still they came, just wanting a taste of the Graduation Boy.

The images began to break apart and melt.

Wesley's head hovering at my crotch like a helium balloon . . .

Jack Devlin's cruel lips opening to eat . . .

the Major's teeth biting down . . .

tongues lapping . . .

throats gorging . . .

wetness . . .

gulping . . .

an endless, oblivious, flow . . .

* * *

"Jesus, what have you done to him? He looks like a zombie!"

"Don't worry, Mr. B., lots of young wild cows have this reaction at their first milking sessions."

"But I had big plans for him this evening. I was going to tongue-plug him, for God's sake!"

"No problem, Mr. B., after a few hours' rest he'll be up and raring to go again. By 9:00 or 9:30 tonight this little studcow will be ready to feed you more than you can drink."

"But he doesn't look like he's got a drop of cum left in him."

"Listen, Clay, Teddy's a natural milkcow. We haven't even begun to tap the reserves of crudeoil in this boy. You're a lucky man to have this gusher all to yourself. I think he could get to be a quart-a-day man. We'll let him rest for a while in the stock lounge and then have him brought up. It's room 27, isn't it?"

excerpt from
THE MILK FARM
MEMBERS' HANDBOOK

Pump Service

The Milk Farm uses vacu-pump techniques to keep the teats of the mancows in full plump condition. A few cows are pumped on a permanent, continuous schedule to increase their teats and milkbags to extraordinary dimensions. Our vacu-pump technicians are also available for Hotel Room Service calls. A Pumper will give only light, recreational pumping to a client and the client should not expect a significant increase in genital size. Nipples may also be pumped, but no pumping of the cocklips will be permitted in Room Service pumping. That specialized process is carried out only in our Labs for Farm stock.

Fuck Service

No assfucking or rimming of Milk Farm staff or cowstock is permitted. Staff and mancows wear assplugs while on duty. These are removed from the cows only when prostate stimulation is required for special milking sessions in the 5-6-7 Milking Suite. Clients are encouraged to visit The Fuck Corral nearby where Pro Fuckers and Asses are available: limousines will transport clients there and back upon request. The Milk Farm does, however, provide late-night Fuck Service by its Security Staff Guards, all of whom have had training at The Corral. The Guards are designated P-8 through P-13 according to equipment dimensions. Clients requiring a more thorough work-out may enquire at the front desk about volunteering for an evening of service bound on the fuck racks in the game room at the guards' barracks.

CHAPTER TEN

Scenes from Life Down on The Farm

Teddy's getting pumped. Daddy's getting plugged. It's ten o'clock on a Saturday night in Room 27 at The Milk Farm Hotel.

Teddy is stretched, his tied wrists pulled up over his head by a rope threaded over the wheel of the pulley in the ceiling at the foot of the bed and running back across the room where it is secured to a screw-eye in the wall behind, keeping him taut. His feet are on the floor, but he doesn't hang vertically: his legs have been spread and pulled back, his ankle cuffs chained to flat rings embedded in the floor, hidden there under removable squares of the carpet for just such a purpose. Teddy's nude body, its young muscles straining, is arched in a voluptuous line with his cock pointing down toward the floor just at the center of the curve, like an arrowhead on a tight bowstring. But his big arrow is not free: the fat pink spear of boyflesh has been inserted into a clear lucite cylinder which is attached to a hollow tube running down to the humming electric vacu-pump on the floor below. Teddy's teenage meat is getting a gentle plumping up from the sweet pulsing pull of the vacuum. His head hangs down, his eyes closed in half-drugged pleasure; a bit of spit drools from the corner of his full rosy lips. He is a pretty sight.

But his daddy Clay is not in much shape to appreciate this vision. He is kneeling on the bed, facing toward the boy, with his wrists in cuffed chains attached to the two corners. His mouth is crammed with a leather dildo-gag and his head has been pulled brutally back by its hair so that he will arch and thrust out his butt to receive the lunges of his assailant. Daddy's getting mean-fucked by Milk Farm Security Guard P-10, or Ripper, as he likes to be called.

Teddy also has his attendant, a short, chunky man with a completely shaven head, who circles him intently, occasionally squatting down at the pump to adjust the pressure so the lad's cock doesn't get too much expansion on its first experience with the

machine. This is one of The Milk Farm's vacu-tech specialists; his name, when he's working on the teats of the mancows in the Labs is Mike, but when he is called to a guest room for client service he introduces himself simply as the Pumper.

The Ripper and the Pumper have been ordered up to start the evening's pleasures: Clay Brock has plans for Teddy's well-sucked cock which require some physical and mental preparation on both their parts.

When the Pumper arrived at the room with his equipment over an hour ago, Clay explained to him that Teddy had been "tried out" in The Milking Barn that afternoon and had been drained dry by the clients who enjoyed an occasional change from the carefully groomed manstock normally available in The Milking Barn stalls. This evening, Clay told the Pumper, he intended to push Teddy as far as he would go, draw out those untapped reserves of milk which an eighteen-year old pup like Teddy undoubtedly had hidden away. And he was going to get that milk by way of the special milking procedure called "Tongue Plugging." But before Teddy could be successfully tongue-plugged certain temporary alterations to his cock had to be made. That was when Clay showed the Pumper the small penis-plug he had already inserted into the cumhole on Teddy's moist glans. The little bullet-shaped rubber stopper was stretching out the first half-inch of Teddy's cumtube so that later Clay's tongue could do its work there at the crucial moments of the milking.

Now, with the small rubber cock-cork still inserted, the pump is causing the whole shaft and head of Teddy's penis to swell and rise like dough, ready to be worked by strong hands and insistent sucking lips.

The Pumper is an expert at his vocation, but he also has that obsessive pre-occupation of his breed: for him BIGGER is always BETTER, and no cock can get too long, no shaft too thick, no glans too swollen, no cumhole too wide, no balls too heavy. If he could, he'd pump every cock and every pair of nuts in the world, make every man alive walk around with several pounds of meat massed into the jock supporters under their bulging trousers. Like many of his kind, the Pumper's godlike tampering with nature's proportions have made him a little mad: he lives in a world of fantastic sexual images and outrageous, obscene propositions. As he

circles around the boy whose cock he is altering, even though only temporarily, he croons a lewd litany of threats and promises.

"Pump you up *big*, Baby. Fifteen, sixteen, maybe *twenty* inches. Get it so long and spongy a fucker can reach around and *wrap it around his hand*, to hang onto while he porks your ass. Pump your balls, Sweetmeat. Big, like grapefruit, like *cantaloupes*. Get you so big you'll need a size 80 jock pouch and a harness to hold 'em up. Pump those pretty little cocklips, too, swell 'em up fat and red, so a sucker can get his teeth on 'em and nibble on your cumhole till you scream. Oh, yeah, Boy, I'll do you good." He continues to circle Teddy's arched body, stopping occasionally to pat and stroke his ass, his pecs, his thighs, to lift his head and look into Teddy's glazed eyes.

On the bed Clay is starting to yelp even more loudly behind his gag. He'd called the front desk for a Fucker, but maybe he'd ordered up more than he could handle. At The Milk Farm fucking isn't a specialty, but the management knows many of its clients cannot live by manmilk alone; they need some sausage-stuffing from time to time as well. So every Security Guard at the resort is also a Fucker, trained at The Fuck Corral to give full professional service on call. All of them have code designations, like Guard P-10, grinding now into Clay's asshole. The P stands for prick, the 10, for the number of inches hard it swells in the client's ass. This is the first time that Clay has ever had the nerve to try a P-10, but he wants to get himself as hot and raunchy as he can for the coming ravishment of Teddy's pumped meat.

The Ripper is just finishing up one of his best sequences, learned during his indoctrination at The Corral: thrusting into the mancunt spread out in front of him with short, jabbing moves, just pushing the head of his pole past the tight sphincter ring until it catches on the wide ledge of his glans, then pulling sharply out, letting the head pop loose like a stopper. He does three of these thrust-and-pop moves, in a steady one-two-three rhythm, then plunges the whole ten-inch torpedo fast and deep in one brutal push, grinding his pubes against the manpussy's tailbone. He pulls out quickly, pauses an instant, then repeats the whole sequence— three urgent thrust-and-pops and one vicious deep jab-and-grind. This goes on and on until he tires of the series, and moves on to something different, a set of deep punches, followed by the slow

pulsing flex of his cock held motionless in the warm canal. The Ripper is "rhythm fucking" in the best Fuck Corral style, and he's got plenty of riffs left in his repertory to try out in this pussy's hole. The Ripper doesn't talk, except with his cock: he just grunts as he pushes in, and growls when Clay responds with muffled squeals.

The Pumper adjusts the vacuum pressure a little, bringing it up more than perhaps he should in a first session, but the kid is getting him feverish with dreams and ideas. He pops small suction cups on the boy's nipples and squeezes them repeatedly, creating little vacuums which pull the tit nubs out into tiny red beads.

"Pump your tits, too. Bring 'em up like juicy strawberries, tie 'em off with cords and tweak 'em 'til they swell like plums. Get my pump on this pouty boymouth. Puff up these ripe lips, maybe even pump up your tongue, give you a big fat dicktongue so you can fuck my asshole with it. Put my pump on your little rosebud boyhole, suck that soft pink lining out so I can rub my dickhead on it. Pump these fat little earlobes, give your face-fuckers something to hold onto. Shoot so much juice on those tonsils, you'll get hoarse. I'll make you talk dirty to me in your wet cum-voice, beat your balls if you ever say anything but *'eat me, feed me, fuck me.'*"

On the bed the Ripper has decided it's time to blast this cunt. He starts his final assault, using the vicious upward thrusts and the brutal corkscrew drilling that have given him his name. Clay's body jolts and writhes under the onslaught.

Keeping up a torment of squeezes and twists on Teddy's balls which dangle invitingly below the clear cocktube, the Pumper squats down, reaches his other hand toward the humming machine, and turns the pressure control up just a little higher.

* * *

It's eleven o'clock and Daddy's lying back on the bed, stroking his cock, his body suffused with the satisfaction of having been well and truly fucked. He feasts his eyes on Teddy's red, turgid hose swaying heavily from his groin.

* * *

The Ripper has gone, after cleaning his cock in the bath of Clay's mouth and blow-drying it in the warm breath from Clay's lungs. The fuck-charge has already been added to Clay's bill and

In the adjacent building, the Punishment Block, Lifeguard Sean's attitude readjustment isn't over yet. The Major slowly gives the handle of the ballpress squeezing Sean's nuts one more quarter-turn. At the same time he advances the gauge on the meter connected to the electrodes pinched onto Sean's cock to a higher level. He keeps the pointer at the new reading until he hears Sean finally articulate the words, "Thank you, Sir!" in the midst of his panting squeals, then lets it drop back down the scale a bit to give the Lifeguard a little breathing space. The Major has decided that Sean is a prime candidate for transfer to one of the private compounds maintained by the billionaire clients on the island called The Last Resort. Handsome lifeguards are a dime a dozen, but a stud who can maintain a stiff cock while his balls are getting pressed and his meat is getting zapped is worth his weight in gold.

＊　＊　＊

In the Studcow Dormitory the Gypsy from the 5-6-7 Box is sunk in a deep dreamless sleep. Rusty is thinking about the young guy who pulled him today—what was his name?—Teddy, that's it—the kid had something special about him—maybe he'll get to plug that sweet mouth again sometime. The Gusher lies spooned against the Milk Shaker; they're pals and they can both feel their enormous reserves of manmilk start to replenish inside them, ready for service the day after tomorrow. The cow who was dried out with ten straight milkings wakes suddenly with a raging hardon; it's like he's suddenly come back to life. He gets out of his bed and moves to the next bunk, straddles the sleeper there, and forces his meat down the half-willing mouth, desperate to prove once again that he's a real shooter.

＊　＊　＊

Next door, in the Hotel Staff Dorm the Nut Boy stirs restlessly; his balls are wrapped in an icepack because it's been an especially hard day—lots of customers didn't like his cocky attitude and took it out on his big firm eggs. Bingo, the swimsuit Boy dreams that a handsome client has offered to buy up his contract and take him on a world tour and the Sauceboy from the Restaurant lies wide awake, worried about the scowl the Major gave him when he crawled out from under the table after gagging on the man's

strong, oily cum. He know it's no good to get the Major on your case. The Cocktail Room Waiter has a sudden flash of inspiration and reaches for the notebook he keeps by his bed. He jots down an idea for a new drink—a Mai-Tai made with almond flavored cum and served by a boy with a round of sliced fresh pineapple slipped over his cockhead for the customer to nibble on between sips. The Management encourages staff initiative and the Cocktail Waiter has his eye on the Bartender's job in the main lounge.

* * *

In his office at the Hotel, Manager Jack Devlin goes over the day's billing. The current crop of clients are good spenders, with a taste for the higher-priced extras like Trainers and service from Staff members with black neck and wrist straps. Hell, one bastard has even booked Devlin himself for a milking tomorrow afternoon. He'll give the sucker a mouthfuck to remember! Beneath his desk his favorite Room Boy licks at his balls, waiting for the main event to begin. Later he'll make the kid beg to be fucked and then he'll fuck him until the kid will beg him to stop, but by then nobody will be able to understand what he's saying because Max, The Farm's Chief of Security will have both of his bull balls *and* his thick meat crammed into the sucker's face. Devlin and Max like working the staff boys over together—they make a good team!

* * *

Upstairs in his room Wesley finishes writing up his Tasting Journal for all the day's pulls. He pages back through earlier entries, remembering fondly some vintage milkings—there was the guy whose cum was grainy and sweet, like a thick Greek rice pudding —and the Latino whose juice was like a succulent meat gravy— and the first pull he did on a young guy whose precum had a lemony tang followed by a cumspray fizz that tasted of creamsoda. Wesley looks at his bedside clock and then swallows his sedative. In a few minutes the Night Nurser will arrive—maybe he'll ask the guy to sprinkle a little cinnamon on his teat before he sinks it into Wesley's smacking lips.

* * *

Across the hall Carlo lies on his stomach with a pillow under his crotch, elevating his classic butt against Ian's slow cock probe. Beneath Carlo's cheek are warm mounds of flesh, the soft thighs of the Pillow Boy they have ordered for the night. Ian is giving his partner one of his all-night fucks. He gently rocks his hard tube into Carlo's hole until he's just ready to cum; then he pulls out and cools down until he's ready for the next bout of long-dicking. Sometime before morning he won't be able to hold off any longer and he'll crawl up and shoot his cum on the Pillow Boy's cock and balls, letting Carlo lick and nuzzle the spermy crotch until he falls asleep.

*　　*　　*

In their dimly lit room Clay moves to sit on the floor beneath Teddy's bloated cock. He takes it in his hand and milks it down, squeezing the head to see if the cumslit has been widened enough for the pleasure he's planned. The puffy cocklips pout open and he sticks his little finger in the dilated hole, probing. He stretches his head up to lick the spicy thread of golden sex-oil that spins out.

"How're you doing, Teddy?" he asks. "Not feeling any pain, are you, kid?"

Teddy opens his eyes and looks down at his stepdad. He's still hanging from the wrist cuffs. He shakes his head and makes a small noise in his throat.

"Ready for some more fun, baby? Going to thank me for such a nice graduation weekend with a big load of buttermilk?"

Two hours ago, when he was still played-out from his repeated milking in the Barn, Teddy would have laughed at the suggestion that he could shoot again tonight. But after the encounter with the Pumper he feels strangely renewed and the flush of lust begins to rise from his groin to his face. About 15 minutes into the pumping session he'd begun to lose the anger and the feeling of betrayal which had overtaken him when Clay had strung him up like a side of beef at the foot of the bed. Watching Clay have a black prick-gag shoved into his mouth and seeing him shafted by the punishing cock of the Ripper, Teddy began to perceive the evening in a new light. The soft, insistent pull of the vacuum on his own prick ceased to be a humiliation and became a kind of pulsating caress. The atmosphere of violence and exploitation that both abused and

excited him was transformed into a heady fog of shared carnal passion. The Pumper's sadistic invocations had spiralled around him, dizzying him with their mad excess.

And now, as Clay releases him and carries him to the bed, promising to take him to another limit of sexual performance, Teddy realizes that the whole weekend has been a series of constantly opening mental doors and constantly expanding sensual experience. And he sees clearly and astonishingly that he has never faltered, moving eagerly through each door as it opened, never turning away from the sometimes frightening visions of sexual fulfillment that each new world has offered.

"I won't tie you this time," murmurs Clay as he places Teddy on the bed and pushes his legs apart so that he can kneel between them for his final rite at the altar of Teddy's groin.

"No," Teddy whispers, "I want you to tie me down. Spread me out and milk me until there's nothing left for me to give."

* * *

Clay pulls at the tumid cock with slow, loving strokes of his lips. He's just tasted a spurt of bittersweet lube, forecasting the climax that is to come after a long, hypnotic suck. He keeps a firm grip on Teddy's balls with one hand, waiting for that tightening that signals the rising of the milk in the cumtube. Teddy takes a deep shuddering breath and holds it as his body stiffens and his groin lifts off the bed pushing the trembling cock deeper into Clay's throat. Clay hardens the end of his tongue, shaping it into a triangular point, and plugs it down solidly into Teddy's wide cumhole. Sperm explodes up the shaft of Teddy's dick, hits against the tongue plugging its opening and surges back into the channel. Each convulsion of his cock and balls sends more juice up the tube, building up an exquisite pressure as it tries to get out. Clay has taken a firm grip with both hands on the quivering meat and the erupting balls as Teddy strains against his bonds.

Finally the jerks and the spasms recede and Clay circles Teddy's shaft tightly with his thumb and forefinger just below the coronal ridge of the glans. This keeps the milk compressed in the stalk of Teddy's boyteat. Now Clay gingerly draws the hard tip of his tongue out of the closed cumhole. He is ready for the ritual.

He releases the pressure of his thumb and forefinger on the shaft

for just a second, just long enough to let a drop of the compressed milk ooze out. Then he re-tightens his grip immediately, keeping the rest of the juice in the tube. Once again he digs his tongue down into the widened mouth of Teddy's cockhead, this time to lap out the drop of cum so that he can spread it all over the swollen plum of flesh, coating the whole surface with slow, lascivious strokes. He releases another drop of the intoxicating liquor and again tongue-paints the head of the cock. Teddy's meatus is agonizingly sensitive, because it has been denied the full release of its load, and the repeated tongue-brushing keeps him in a state of unrelenting orgasmic frenzy for the half-hour it takes until all the rich custard has been freed, drop by drop from the finger-squeezed tube.

Teddy is moaning continuously now, lost in a trance of frustrated desire. Then the milk is completely gone and Teddy sinks back relaxed and contented.

But Clay immediately takes the still engorged meat firmly in his fist, grips the spent balls tightly and jacks the shaft roughly up and down, willing the boy to produce another flow of seed. Within seconds he spurts again, his eyes wide with wonder at the unlimited reservoirs of cum which seem to flood from within him. Clay plugs, squeezes, releases, and strokes in the same tormenting ritual of denied climax as before, only now the head of Teddy's cock has become so acutely and deliriously alive that he faints from the glut of pleasure that inundates him. Clay feels the body beneath him relax into unconsciousness. He lets his hand go slack around the cock he is worshipping and draws the last of the nectar out in one long insatiable drink.

Teddy has been kept in an almost constant state of orgasm for nearly an hour. His stay as a guest at The Milk Farm is complete. He is ready for the next door and the next world.

* * *

Late on Sunday morning Teddy wakes from a sleep so profound that coming out of it is like being reborn. A note from Clay lies on the pillow beside him.

I've gone to the Wild Cow Pull. You can watch it on Channel 6 if you like. Order breakfast in but don't leave the room. Your cock was sweet this morning. I licked it for an hour before I got up. Clay

He orders juice, cereal, bacon, eggs, toast, muffins, and every-thing else he can think of, and settles back against the pillows. Drowsily, he pushes the button on the TV remote for channel 6. The Wild Cow Pull is like a weird orgy directed by some crazed film director. An intake of new cow stock had been delivered to The Farm the day before. Now the men are being offered to Farm clients as "wild milk"—untrained, unconditioned teats getting their first experience of what they can expect during their life at The Farm. The scene is bedlam. Guys tied down to tables and benches. Strapped to pillars and railings. Blindfolded, some gagged. Yell-ing, screaming, cursing, whimpering. Clients slavering over the new meat. Pulling greedily at raw, virgin dicks, some of which may have never known a man's mouth before. Milk Farm staff move about the big receiving room flicking leather crops and whips on the flanks, the asses, and the nipples of the new stock to bring them to greater panic pitch. In one corner a figure is hunched over the crotch of a slender kid with a blonde crew cut, a hairless body, and a small dick and balls. It is Clay, eating him whole, stuffing both meat and nuts into his mouth at once. The kid's blindfolded face is thrown back in a howl of fury and rapture.

Teddy's eyes have closed on the apocalyptic scene and he's asleep again when the Room Waiter comes in to leave the heav-ily laden tray. The waiter stands by the bed, staring at the images of the Wild Cow orgy, then looks at the sleeping boy. His mouth drags down at the corners in a sardonic grin.

*　*　*

CONTRACT

The Milk Farm agrees to take possession of Theodore (Teddy) Brock for a period of three years, with an option for another two years at the discretion of The Milk Farm Management. In return Clay Brock will receive, at the end of the three year period, certain documents, photographs, and video tapes currently in the possession of The Pleasure Corporation, the parent company of The Milk Farm. In addi-tion Clay Brock will receive a free membership in The Farm and be entitled to a discount of 50% on all fees and charges during the period of the agreement.

By signing this CONTRACT Clay Brock agrees that his stepson shall be trained, conditioned, maintained and offered for use by The Farm

Management as a STOCK COW in Milking Barn stall-service. Further Clay Brock understands that The Milk Farm retains the rights to all income arising from the offering of these services, and also from the sale of any Utility Sperm drawn from the subject in mechanical milking devices. After the initial six-week orientation period, the Management agrees that Clay Brock shall have "first pull" privileges on Teddy Brock, and that on visits to The Farm Clay Brock shall have the use of Teddy in his Hotel room, as well as in The Milking Barn. The sole condition of this proviso is that Clay Brock agrees that he will not spoil the potential for later sale and use of Teddy Brock by penetrating him anally during any of these visits.

By signing this CONTRACT Clay Brock understands and agrees that certain physical modifications may be made to his stepson's physique, especially to his genitals and to his sperm production system. The enlargement of sexual organs and amplification of semen volume may be continued to any extent and dimension deemed desirable by the Management.

Should the Management of The Milk Farm choose not to exercise its Option Rights to a further two-year term of service, it is understood that Clay Brock agrees to the transfer of the Option Rights to any one of three other Pleasure Corporation branches: The SbarM Ranch, The Cock and Ball Restaurant, or The Fuck Corral.

Because this Contract has no force in law, it is to be understood that enforcement of the Penalty Proviso below will be carried out by The Pleasure Corporation Security Division.

PENALTY PROVISO: CLAY BROCK AGREES, BY SIGNING THIS CONTRACT, THAT ANY REFUSAL OF TEDDY BROCK TO PARTICIPATE FULLY AND WITHOUT HESITATION IN THE ACTIVITIES OF THE MILK FARM WILL RESULT IN HIS BEING ASSIGNED TO ANY OTHER DUTIES OR BRANCHES OF THE PLEASURE CORPORATION AS THE MANAGEMENT SEES FIT. FURTHER, CLAY BROCK AGREES THAT IN THE EVENT TEDDY BROCK LEAVES THE PREMISES WITHOUT AUTHORIZATION, HE HIMSELF WILL BE BROUGHT TO THE FARM TO SERVE IN HIS STEAD UNTIL SUCH TIME AS TEDDY BROCK IS RETURNED.

The CONTRACT is entirely conditional on the agreement of Theodore Brock to its stipulation. It will be shown to him and he will be given ample opportunity to refuse employment or to ask that certain terms be altered.

Upon the signing of the CONTRACT Clay Brock will be given one

hour with his stepson in the privacy of their Milk Farm Hotel room to acquaint Teddy with the terms of this contract, after which time, Teddy Brock, on his agreement, will be removed to the staff compound for the commencement of his training as a MILK FARM STOCK COW.

SIGNED THIS DAY OF _____, IN THE YEAR OF _____

BY _____

    JACK DEVLIN, MANAGER OF THE MILK FARM AND
    REPRESENTATIVE OF THE PLEASURE CORPORATION

AND _____

    CLAY BROCK, GUARDIAN OF THEODORE BROCK

AND _____

    THEODORE BROCK

※   ※   ※

It is three o'clock on a Sunday afternoon in Room 27 of The Milk Farm Hotel. Clay Brock shows the Contract to Teddy and tries to explain why he has had to sign it. Teddy is impassive, his face showing no expression. Clay sits down on the bed beside the boy and puts his arm around his shoulders. He begins to apologize for suggesting that Teddy sign away his freedom. Teddy shrugs off the embrace and pushes away the hand that has been inching up his thigh toward his groin. He is tired of Clay now. He walks to the balcony doors and stands looking out.

He thinks of the pearl of sperm that made the milker drunk for months after he swallowed it.

He has a fleeting sensation of whirling, with his cock lashing about in spasms of release.

The Honeyboy's face . . . *Tim* . . . flickers and holds in his mind.

He wishes the guards would come to take him to the new adventures that await.

CHAPTER ELEVEN

Addenda to *The Milk Farm E-Mail File*

OUTGOING E-MAIL FILE
Manager, The Milk Farm
TO: CHIEF@PolHead.priv.
FROM: MGRJack@MFarm.priv.
[Encrypted message]
URGENT!
Chief:

I am sorry to have to report to you that last evening your nephew Tim and an accomplice, Teddy Brock, left The Milk Farm without authorization. A check of the area by our Security Division has failed to locate them, so we now must treat them as runaways. As you well know it is imperative that they be returned to The Farm, both for security reasons, and because their escape constitutes a considerable loss of assets. Tim is one of our most requested milkcows and Teddy Brock was just completing his six-week orientation and conditioning program. Although we knew the boys had become friends, we had no warning that they planned to escape.

I must confess that we now know that Tim may have been allowed to read, by accident, a report on the desk of the Lab Director that recommended he be given experimental milk enhancement hormones which also trigger the subject's libido to such an extent that he has to be kept in permanent restraint. I assure you that we had no intention of actually engaging in such an experiment on Tim and we have disciplined the Director accordingly.

I have to ask you to mobilize our Milk Farm friends on the Police Force to conduct a thorough search of likely places in the city where they may be hiding. We suspect they may approach Clay Brock or even go to the house of Teddy's mother. It is also possible, of course, that some local client of The Farm has taken them in: I attach here a list of such addresses, but I urge you to conduct enquiries with discretion.

If and when the two boys are found, they should be returned to the custody of The Milk Farm Security Division immediately.

Jack

* * *

INCOMING E-MAIL FILE
Manager, The Milk Farm
TO: MGRJack@MFarm.priv.
FROM: CHIEF@PolHead.priv.
[Encrypted message]
Jack:
What the hell is going on out there?!

I'll do what I can from here, but it's a big town and there are only a few officers we can trust with this duty. If we do find these two, I intend to keep Tim with me. Even though his Contract with you is not finished, I want to start using him on a regular basis myself. We'll send Teddy Brock back to you as requested.

You'd better get your so-called Security Division on the stick!

The Chief

* * *

OUTGOING E-MAIL FILE
Manager, The Milk Farm
TO: CEO.PleasCorp@Head.priv.
FROM: MGRJack@MFarm.priv.
[Encrypted message]
Dear Sir:
It has now been one month since the two stock cows went missing from The Farm and since our chances of finding them are becoming slimmer by the day, we should begin to consider our courses of action against the original signers of their Contracts, Clay Brock and The Chief. Both Contracts contain the standard Penalty Proviso allowing for the replacement of the lost stock by the signers themselves, but I wish to have your advice before I proceed.

Jack

* * *

INCOMING E-MAIL FILE
    Manager, The Milk Farm
TO: MGRJack@MFarm.priv.
FROM: CEO.PleasCorp@Head.priv.
[Encrypted message]
Dear Jack:
Take Clay Brock into immediate custody using either the Chief's resources or our own Security Division. He should be kept in the guards' barracks, where he may be used as a Utility Boy until we arrange for his transfer to The Last Resort. The matter of sanctions against The Chief is more delicate and will be considered at the next Board meeting, to be held in Budapest later this month at the time of the opening of the new Cock and Ball Restaurant there. At that meeting the Board will also discuss the disciplinary measures necessary for your own failure to provide satisfactory security at The Farm.

> "Sporus"
> Chief Executive Officer
> The Pleasure Corporation

(sign on the bulletin board of The Milk Farm security barracks)

The new temporary Utility Boy is a former Milk Farm Client
known to the staff as Mr. B. His new name is
Suckbutt.
He is to be kept chained to the wall
of the Barracks Playroom and is on 24-hour call
pending his transfer to The Last Resort as a
V.A.P.S.
(Volunteer All-Purpose Slave)

AIDS RISK REDUCTION GUIDELINES
FOR HEALTHIER SEX

As given by Bay Area Physicians for Human Rights

NO RISK: *Most of these activities involve only skin-to-skin contact, thereby avoiding exposure to blood, semen, and vaginal secretions. This assumes there are no breaks in the skin.* 1) **Social kissing** (dry). 2) **Body massage, hugging.** 3) **Body to body rubbing** (frottage). 4) **Light S&M** (without bruising or bleeding). 5) **Using one's own sex toys.** 6) **Mutual masturbation** (male or external female). Care should be taken to avoid exposing the partners to ejaculate or vaginal secretions. Seminal, vaginal and salivary fluids should not be used as lubricants.

LOW RISK: *In these activities small amounts of certain body fluids might be exchanged, or the protective barrier might break causing some risk.* 1) **Anal or vaginal intercourse with condom.** Studies have shown that HIV does not penetrate the condom in simulated intercourse. Risk is incurred if the condom breaks or if semen spills into the rectum or vagina. The risk is further reduced if one withdraws before climax. 2) **Fellatio interruptus** (sucking, stopping before climax). Pre-ejaculate fluid may contain HIV. Saliva or other natural protective barriers in the mouth may inactivate virus in pre-ejaculate fluid. Saliva may contain HIV in low concentration. The insertive partner should warn the receptive partner before climax to prevent exposure to a large volume of semen. If mouth or genital sores are present, risk is increased. Likewise, action which causes mouth or genital injury will increase risk. 3) **Fellatio with condom** (sucking with condom) Since HIV cannot penetrate an intact condom, risk in this practice is very low unless breakage occurs. 4) **Mouth-to-mouth kissing** (French kissing, wet kissing) Studies have shown that HIV is present in saliva in such low concentration that salivary exchange is unlikely to transmit the virus. Risk is increased if sores in the mouth or bleeding gums are present. 5) **Oral-vaginal or oral-anal contact with protective barrier.** e.g. a latex dam, obtainable through a local dental supply house, may be used. Do not reuse latex barrier, because sides of the barrier may be reversed inadvertently. 6) **Manual anal contact with glove** (manual anal (fisting) or manual vaginal (internal) contact with glove). If the glove does not break, virus transmission should not occur. However, significant trauma can still be inflicted on the rectal tissues leading to other medical problems, such as hemorrhage or bowel perforation. 7) **Manual vaginal contact with glove** (internal). See above.

MODERATE RISK: *These activities involve tissue trauma and/or exchange of body fluids which may transmit HIV or other sexually transmitted disease.* 1) **Fellatio** (sucking to climax). Semen may contain high concentrations of HIV and if absorbed through open sores in the mouth or digestive tract could pose risk. 2) **Oral-anal contact** (rimming). HIV may be contained in blood-contaminated feces or in the anal rectal lining. This practice also poses high risk of transmission of parasites and other gastrointestinal infections. 3) **Cunnilingus** (oral-vaginal contact). Vaginal secretions and menstrual blood have been shown to harbor HIV, thereby causing risk to the oral partner if open lesions are present in the mouth or digestive tract. 4) **Manual rectal contact** (fisting). Studies have indicated a direct association between fisting and HIV infection for both partners. This association may be due to concurrent use of recreational drugs, bleeding, pre-fisting semen exposure, or anal intercourse with ejaculation. 5) **Sharing sex toys.** 6) **Ingestion of urine.** HIV has not been shown to be transmitted via urine; however, other immunosuppressive agents or infections may be transmitted in this manner.

HIGH RISK: *These activities have been shown to transmit HIV.* 1) **Receptive anal intercourse without condom.** All studies imply that this activity carries the highest risk of transmitting HIV. The rectal lining is thinner than that of the vagina or the mouth thereby permitting ready absorption of the virus from semen or pre-ejaculate fluid to the blood stream. One laboratory study suggests that the virus may enter by direct contact with rectal lining cells without any bleeding. 2) **Insertive anal intercourse without condom.** Studies suggest that men who participate only in this activity are at less risk of being infected than their partners who are rectally receptive; however the risk is still significant. It carries high risk of infection by other sexually transmitted diseases. 3) **Vaginal intercourse without condom.**

BOOKS FROM LEYLAND PUBLICATIONS / G.S PRESS

☐ **PARTINGS AT DAWN: Anthology of Japanese Gay Literature.** Brilliant collection covering 800 years of Japanese culture. Illus. $21.95.

☐ **OUT OF THE BLUE: Russia's Hidden Gay Literature.** 400 page anthology of stories, articles, photos—New Russia & earlier. $21.95.

☐ **THE LEGIONNAIRE.** Erotic novel by Tom Kvaale. $16.95.

☐ **THE MILK FARM.** Erotic novel by Luc Milne. $16.95.

☐ **MUSCLESEX A collection of erotic stories** by Greg Nero. $16.95.

☐ **CRYSTAL BOYS** The first modern Asian gay novel by Pai Hsien-yung $16.95.

☐ **MEN LOVING MEN: A Gay Sex Guide & Consciousness Book** by Mitch Walker. New revised edition. 40 + photos. $16.95.

☐ **MEATMEN Anthology of Gay Male Comics.** Tom of Finland, Donelan, etc. Large sized books. Circle books wanted. Volumes 1, 2, 3, 4, 5, 6, 7, 8, 9, 10, 11, 12, 13, 14, 15, 16—$17.95 ea. Vols. 17, 18, 19—$18.95 ea.

☐ **OH BOY! Sex Comics** by Brad Parker. $12.95.

☐ **ENLISTED MEAT / WARRIORS & LOVERS / MILITARY SEX / MARINE BIOLOGY / BASIC TRAINING: True Homosexual Military Stories.** $16.95 each. Circle books wanted. Soldiers / sailors / marines tell all about their sex lives.

☐ **SEX BEHIND BARS / BOYS BEHIND BARS / THE BOYS OF VASELINE ALLEY** (3 Vols.) by Robert N. Boyd. $16.95 each. Circle books wanted.

☐ **MANPLAY / YOUNG NUMBERS / BOYS BOYS BOYS! / STUDFLESH / BOYS WILL BE BOYS / EIGHTEEN & OVER:** True Gay Encounters. Circle books wanted. Hot male-male sex stories. $12.95 each.

☐ **LUST** and **HUMONGOUS** True Gay Encounters. Vols. 1 & 5 $16.95 ea.

☐ **LEATHERMEN SPEAK OUT** Vols. 1 & 2. Ed. Jack Ricardo. 50 leather dads & sons, slaves & masters reveal their S&M sex encounters. $16.95 ea.

☐ **SIR! MORE SIR! The Joy of S&M** by Master Jackson. $16.95.

☐ **THE KISS OF THE WHIP: Explorations in SM** by Jim Prezwalski $17.95.

☐ **KISS FOOT, LICK BOOT.** Foot, Sox, Sneaker & Boot Worship/Domination Stories. Edited by Doug Gaines/The Foot Fraternity. $16.95.

☐ **TRUCKER / SEXSTOP / HOT TRICKS / MEAT RACK:** True sex stories. Circle books wanted. $12.95 each.

☐ **ROUGH TRADE: True Revelations** Vol. 7. Hot sex stories. $16.95

☐ **ROCK ON THE WILD SIDE: Gay Male Images in Popular Music of the Rock Era** by Wayne Studer. Illustrated. $17.95.

☐ **GAY ROOTS: Anthology of Gay History, Sex, Politics & Culture.** 100 + writers. Illustrated. 1000 + pages total. Vol. 1: $25.95; Vol. 2 $22.95.

☐ **HIGH CAMP: A Guide to Gay Cult & Camp Films** by Paul Roen. $17.95.

☐ **AUSSIE BOYS / AUSSIE HOT** by Rusty Winter. $16.95 each.

☐ **MEAT / SEX / CUM / JUICE / CREAM True Homosexual Experiences from S.T.H.** Boyd McDonald $16.95 each (5 vols.). Circle books wanted.

☐ **MILKIN' THE BULLS and other Hot Hazing Stories** by John Barton. Stories of military school, sexual hazing, etc. $16.95.

☐ **ORGASMS / HOT STUDS / SINGLEHANDED:** Homosexual Encounters from *First Hand*. $12.95 each (3 vols.). Circle books wanted.

☐ **GHOST KISSES Gothic Gay Romance Stories** by Gregory Norris $14.95.

TO ORDER: Check book(s) wanted (or list them on a separate sheet) and send check / money order to Leyland Publications, PO Box 410690, San Francisco, CA 94141. **Postage included in prices quoted.** Calif. residents add 8½ % sales tax. Mailed in unmarked book envelopes. Add $1 for complete catalogue.